RIGHT
BESIDE YOU

Published by Kensington Publishing Corp.

RIGHT BESIDE YOU

MARY MONROE

www.kensingtonbooks.com

DAFINA BOOKS are published by

Kensington Publishing Corp.
119 West 40th Street
New York, NY 10018

All Kensington titles, imprints, and distributed lines are available at special quantity discounts for bulk purchases for sales promotion, premiums, fund-raising, educational, or institutional use. Special book excerpts or customized printings can also be created to fit specific needs. For details, write or phone the office of the Kensington Special Sales Manager: Attn. Special Sales Department. Kensington Publishing Corp, 119 West 40th Street, New York, NY 10018. Phone: 1-800-221-2647.

The DAFINA logo is a trademark of Kensington Publishing Corp.

ISBN-13: 978-1-4967-3206-4
ISBN-10: 1-4967-3206-5
First Kensington Hardcover Edition: October 2019
First Kensington Mass Market Edition: October 2021

ISBN-13: 978-1-4967-1585-2 (e-book)
ISBN-10: 1-4967-1585-3 (e-book)

10 9 8 7 6 5 4 3 2 1

Printed in the United States of America

This book is dedicated to my beloved nieces,
Mona Lisa Williams and Sarah Louise Nicholson.

ACKNOWLEDGMENTS

It is such an honor to be a member of the Kensington Books family.

Selena James is an awesome editor and a great friend. Thank you, Selena! Thanks to Steven Zacharius, Adam Zacharius, Karen Auerbach, Vida Engstrand, Lauren Jernigan, Samantha McVeigh, Elizabeth Trout, Robin E. Cook, the wonderful crew in the sales department, and everyone else at Kensington for working so hard for me.

Thanks to Lauretta Pierce for maintaining my website.

Thanks to the fabulous book clubs, bookstores, libraries, my readers, and the magazine and radio interviewers for supporting me for so many years.

To my super literary agent and friend, Andrew Stuart, thank you for representing me with so much vigor.

Please continue to email me at Authorauthor 5409@aol.com and visit my website at www.mary monroe.org. You can also communicate with me on Facebook at Facebook.com/MaryMonroe and Twitter @Mary MonroeBooks.

Peace and Blessings,
Mary Monroe

PROLOGUE
FELICIA

Commuting to and from work by bus five days a week was more enjoyable to me than driving or carpooling. Some of the passengers I rode with were fellow coworkers I liked to network with. However, that was hard to do during business hours. We all had busy jobs and were scattered throughout the building. It was easier to catch up on each other's lives on the bus.

Richard Grimes and I were employees at the same firm, but in different departments. Unless we had to attend a staff meeting, bumped into each other in the elevator, or I needed his tech support assistance, I could go for days without seeing him at the office. Some weeks the only time we saw each other was on our commuter bus. When I didn't see him, I missed him.

Richard and I usually shared the same seat near the rear of the bus where it was easier to kick back and chat. We had a lot in common and never ran out of things to discuss. We had been fellow commuters for several years and had developed a close, platonic relationship. And now, I looked forward to being with him more than the men I dated . . .

CHAPTER 1
FELICIA

November 23rd

I usually wore my shoulder-length, dark brown hair in a style that would enhance my delicate features. But this particular Friday, I'd spent so much time on my couch, lying on my back and shifting from side to side, that my hair was a hot, matted mess. Rather than fuss with it, I had covered my head with a black scarf my cousin Wendell had left at my place a couple of weeks ago.

I was not trying to impress anybody dressed in a bulky sweatshirt and jeans, so it didn't matter that I looked like a frump when I decided to make a trip to Ralph's Market a few minutes after seven p.m. It was only a couple of blocks from my apartment. I didn't think I'd be out long enough to run into anybody I knew.

I was sorry I hadn't put on my earmuffs, muffler, and gloves. Northern Ohio was known for its brutal winters and late November was when it began to get bitterly cold. There was already a thin blanket of snow on the ground, but I knew that as early as next week, the snow could be up to my knees. That was the reason I owned several pairs of thigh-high boots. The ones I had on now had flat heels, so I didn't look as tall as I did in the four-inch Louboutin high heels I owned.

"Excuse me. I'm sorry, ma'am." The deep voice belonged to a man who had accidentally bumped into my shopping cart with his in the health-care products aisle. When I turned around, he did a double take. His eyes widened as if he'd just been frightened. I was so embarrassed I wanted to run out the door.

"Felicia, *is that you?*" His eyes returned to their normal size as he slowly looked me up and down. I couldn't tell from the expression on his finely chiseled, nut-brown face if he was disappointed or amused to see what I really looked like without help from various cosmetics created specifically for women of color. In his black wool overcoat, red muffler, and leather gloves, he looked as dapper as ever. I held my breath as he gently caressed his goatee. This was the first time I'd noticed a few flecks of gray in it, but it still looked distinguished and sophisticated.

"Um, yes. It's me," I replied meekly as I shifted my weight from one foot to the other. The large bottle of Gas-X Extra Strength I had just plucked off the shelf was still in my hand. "How was your Thanksgiving, Richard?" I silently prayed that he wouldn't detain me too long. Richard Grimes and I had been coworkers and commuter bus seat mates for over eight years and he'd never seen the "real" me until now.

"It was great. The girls and I had dinner with the family in Cleveland. And boy, what a feast! Turkey, ham, dressing, collard greens, and all the other trimmings. My mother-in-law bakes such mean sweet potato pies, I ate a whole one by myself." He grinned and patted his stomach. "I'll be counting calories for the next few weeks. How was yours?"

"Mine was great, too. We had a meal fit for a king. My grandmother bakes mean sweet potato pies, too. I ate three slices one right after the other without leaving the table, and enough of everything else to feed an army," I said with a chuckle as I sucked in my stomach.

"Did you make it to any of the Black Friday

sales today? You mentioned doing so a few times on the bus the other day."

"Well, when I thought more about it, the idea didn't sound so appealing anymore. I decided to skip all that chaos this year. I spent most of the day watching holiday programs. This is the first time I left my apartment today."

Richard rolled his sparkling black eyes and continued. "I wish I could say that. I've been in and out of my house all day. With two teenage girls in the house and other female relatives popping in and out, we're always out of something." His cart contained hair products, toiletries, toothpaste, and a huge box of Orville Redenbacher's popcorn.

I got lightheaded when I noticed how he was staring at the items in my cart: corn removers, bunion pads, an enema bag, Poligrip denture adhesive, and a large bag of Cheetos. "Picking up a few things for my grandmother," I quickly explained, gently placing the Gas-X into my cart. I made a mental note to visit the spirits aisle and grab a bottle of wine for myself. After this embarrassing encounter, I would pop it open as soon as I got home.

I rarely ran into any of my coworkers away from the office. I couldn't believe that with all the stores in Mandell, Ohio, I'd ended up at the same one the same time as a coworker when I looked like a frump. And pushing a cart that contained such embarrassing merchandise. If it had been anybody other than Richard, it wouldn't have bothered me. I had never heard him say anything malicious or unflattering about another person, but I didn't want to know what was going through his mind now. No matter what it was, I didn't care because Richard was everything I wanted in a man. He was good-looking, sensitive, responsible, socially active in the community, patient, and stable. He was three years older than me, and very well kept for a forty-year-old man. The most handsome and eligible bachelor I knew had lived in the same house since birth, worked for the same company for fifteen years, and attended the same church on a regular basis. What more could a woman ask for?

This man makes my knees weak. And he had no idea.

I was glad he interrupted my thoughts. "Do you have big plans for the weekend?" he asked.

"Um . . . just more shopping. Christmas is still over a month away, but I have a very long gift list. I don't want to wait too much longer to get started. I still have to find a dress to wear to Marybeth's wedding in January and I'd like to take advantage of some of the amazing end-of-year sales."

"I advise you not to buy one that'll attract too much attention. My cousin Stella wore a dress to my wedding that was so over-the-top, our guests couldn't keep their eyes off her. My bride was not happy about being upstaged on her big day."

"I can understand that. When I get married, I hope another woman doesn't steal my thunder." I rarely said bonehead things. I couldn't believe I'd just mentioned my wedding, because I wasn't even in a serious relationship and hadn't been in *years*.

I was about to excuse myself and go pay for my merchandise when a petite honey-colored woman in a beige wool coat and black leather boots with heels at least three inches high pranced around the corner. Regina Dobbins was the kind of woman who always looked like she belonged on a fashion magazine cover. She stood out in a low-end store like Ralph's Market. Her makeup was flawless. Her thick auburn hair was in a French roll that made her look even more elegant. "Richie, I told you they'd be out of those—" She stopped talking when she spotted me. "Oh, hello." From the confused look on her face, I could tell she didn't recognize me, either.

"Reggie, you know Felicia Hawkins, right? She shared a table with us at our office Fourth of July picnic this year." Richard nodded in my direction.

"Of course, I know Felicia. We had a couple of classes together in high school." There was a reserved look on her face when she added in a sugary-sweet tone, "Are you still engaged to marry that football player?"

Before I could respond, Richard answered. "That's Marybeth. She's part of Felicia's clerical support staff," he explained.

"Oh yeah." Regina paused and glanced at the items in my cart. "Doing some weekend shopping, huh? I didn't attempt to make it to any sales at the big stores today. Black Friday brings out the worst in some people. Dozens of desperate shoppers stormed Walmart before daybreak this morning. What I saw on the news this afternoon scared me to death. The police arrested a woman for pepper-spraying another customer when she tried to cut in line."

"Last year I was one of those desperate shoppers," I admitted dryly. When Regina glanced at my purchases again, this time with her lips scrunched up, I said, "Like I told Richard a few moments ago, I didn't bother with it this year. The only reason I came here this evening was to pick up a few things for my grandmother."

"Guess who else was a desperate shopper this year?" Regina said with a snicker. Then she playfully elbowed Richard's arm and winked at me. "This man stood in a block-long line at Walmart for two hours before daybreak this morning. And all he bought was a new case for his iPhone."

"I didn't see anything else I needed," Richard said in a low voice with a sheepish grin. Then in a firm tone he abruptly told me, "Felicia, I hope you'll enjoy the rest of your evening."

"Thank you. I hope you will, too." I didn't want to ask what he and Regina had planned for later tonight because I didn't want to know. She told me anyway.

"I promised Richard a beer if he'd give me a ride home," she stated. "My car is in the shop, so I took Uber to get here. I was lucky to run into him on my way in. I'm going to try and talk him into going to the Black Tiger bar with me later."

"That's a nice bar, so I know you'll both have a good time," I muttered. I was disappointed to hear about Richard's possible "date" with this gorgeous woman, but I was pleased to see such a woeful look on his face.

CHAPTER 2
RICHARD

Felicia's comment about her getting married was still ringing in my ears. I was still so surprised that a woman like her wasn't already married . . .

"Richard, what's the matter? Why did you get so quiet and glassy-eyed all of a sudden?" Regina asked in a concerned tone as she shook my arm.

"Huh? Oh! I was just trying to remember if there was anything else I needed to pick up," I fumbled. "I'm fine." I gave her a tight, fake smile. I was glad she'd interrupted my thoughts. But as soon as she started chatting with Felicia again, my mind wandered off in another direction anyway.

I spent time with several different women, but Regina Dobbins was the one folks saw me with the most. I had dated her in high school and we had taken our relationship to the next level during our four years at Ohio State. We'd planned to have a future together. She'd balked when I told her I wanted to do a stint in the army before I settled down. But she wanted to stay in the relationship anyway. We got together every time I came home on leave and we corresponded by letter on a weekly basis. However, six months before my discharge, she stopped answering my letters. I called her a few times from Iraq and was never able to reach her. Finally, two months before my discharge, she sent the "Dear John" letter that ended our engagement—in the same envelope with the announcement of her upcoming wedding. By the time I returned home, she and her new husband had moved to Alaska. Less than a year later, I met a wonderful woman named Margaret Pritchard at a church fundraiser. I married her eight months later. While I was on my honeymoon, Regina's husband divorced her and she returned to Mandell.

Five years ago, when my daughters were eight and nine, Margaret was diagnosed with uterine cancer. It was so aggressive, she died three months after her diagnosis. I was devastated.

Somehow, I recovered and started dating

again four months after the funeral. Regina and I still socialized with some of the same mutual friends, so we'd bump into each other from time to time, always with other dates. When we finally ended up without dates at the same neighborhood cookout one weekend, we decided to start going out again. She wanted a more serious and permanent relationship. So did I, but not with her. The main reason was because she had no desire to have children, which was why her husband had divorced her. I wanted to have at least one more, so we could never have a future together.

I still had feelings for her and I enjoyed her company. But I'd made it clear from the get-go that I would still see other women. She spent time with other men as well.

Regina must not have noticed that I'd become distracted again. I could hear her and Felicia talking, but it sounded like gibberish to me. I shook my head to clear my thoughts. "It was nice seeing you, Felicia. I'll see you on the bus next week," I told her.

"Bye, Richard, Regina. Have a blessed night," she replied.

I walked through the checkout line and out the store in a daze. Even though Regina had looped her arm through mine, I had almost forgotten she was with me. That's the kind of effect Felicia Hawkins had on me.

We tossed our bags into the back seat of my Ford Explorer, and we got in and fastened our seat belts. I pulled out of the parking lot and eased onto the busy street before either one of us spoke again. "She's nice," Regina said.

"She who?" I asked dumbly.

Regina whirled around to face me with her mouth hanging open. "Richard, you're beginning to scare me. What is the matter with you tonight?"

"I'm fine. Just anxious to get out of this cold weather," I answered as I reached to turn on the heater.

"Anyway, I was talking about Felicia."

"She is nice," I agreed.

"She was so popular with the boys in our school. I wonder which one married her."

"She's never been married," I said quickly. Traffic was heavy, so I kept my eyes on the road. But from the corner of my eye, I noticed a curious look on Regina's face.

She shifted in her seat and looked away. "That's a shame. I wonder why." Then she added with a chuckle, "She's very attractive when she's fixed up."

"I think she's very attractive even when she's not 'fixed up,'" I defended.

Regina sucked in some air and went on. "Are we going to the Black Tiger later so I can buy that beer I owe you?"

"I'll take a rain check. I limit myself to only four drinks a week and I filled that quota yesterday at my in-laws' dinner."

"If you change your mind, let me know."

When I parked in front of the large red brick house Regina had recently purchased, I was surprised to see that every light in her house was on. Her baby sister, Diana, who had come up from Toledo for Thanksgiving and was going to stay until after Christmas, was peeping out the front window. "That girl. My light bill is going to be sky-high this month," Regina griped. "I love her to death, but I don't know if I can stand to have her around for a whole month. That's why I wanted to get out of the house tonight."

"I felt the same way when my cousin Mike stayed at my house the whole Christmas week last year. But I missed him when he left and I'm sure you'll feel the same way about Diana when she leaves."

"You're right and I feel guilty because I did invite her. Hey! Why don't we get one of your friends for her and let's go out tomorrow night.

Or some other night real soon. I don't want to wait for it to get too close to Christmas when all the bars will be so crowded."

"Let me get back to you about that. I have a lot of things planned to do with my girls in the next few weeks."

"Oh. Well, tell Marva and Carol their auntie Regina said hello."

When I pulled into the driveway of the huge white stucco house I'd inherited from my parents, my elder daughter, fourteen-year-old Marva, flung open the front door as soon as I walked up on the porch. Thirteen-year-old Carol stood behind her. With their cute cinnamon-colored faces, petite frames, and wavy black hair, they looked so much like their mother. They had already put on their pajamas and I planned to do the same thing myself as soon as I could.

"What took you so long?" Marva asked. She grabbed my arm and led me into our spacious, lavishly furnished living room. My wife had taken her last breath on the couch we'd owned back then. Because of that, my in-laws could no longer stand to look at it. So my Christmas present from them that year was the plush lavender couch and matching love seat in our living room now. Marva had picked out the purple and black brocade curtains at the living-room windows. "Daddy, while you were gone, we vacuumed every floor, cleaned our bathroom—and yours—and we put all the Thanksgiving food we brought home from Grandma's yesterday in baggies and put them in the freezer."

"And you didn't even have to tell us to do all that this time," Carol pointed out. She and her sister had learned their good housekeeping skills from their mother, so our beautiful two-story house was always so neat and spotless, sometimes it didn't even look lived in. I was happy to see that they also had a nice blaze going in the fireplace. "Did you get lost or run into one of your friends? We didn't know you'd be gone so long."

"I ran into Regina. After I had finished all my shopping, I had to wait until she finished hers so I could give her a ride home," I replied.

"Again?" Carol said, rolling her eyes.

"Her car is in the shop," I explained.

"And she just happened to be in the market the same time as you, like the last two times?"

"That's not so unusual. A lot of folks in this part of town shop at Ralph's Market because it's convenient," I declared. "What's the big deal, Carol?"

"Daddy, that lady is trying to set you up. Like last year when she just happened to have an extra ticket to the Cavaliers game and talked you into going with her."

A self-satisfied smile crossed my face. "Everybody knows that's my favorite team. I hadn't been able to get a ticket myself so I was glad to go with her," I reminded.

Both girls rolled their eyes this time.

"Did you get everything?" Marva asked, pulling on one of the shopping bags in my hand.

"Everything except the green apples. They were all out." I paused and glanced around the room. "Homework done?"

"I'm done!" Carol shouted with a thumbs-up.

"I'm almost done," Marva muttered, looking at the floor.

"Make sure you finish it before you get on that computer or start fiddling around with your phone," I advised with a stern look.

While they rifled through the two shopping bags, I removed my coat and hung it on the rack by the door. With a deep sigh, I flopped down on the couch and removed my boots. It had been a humdrum day for me until my encounter with Felicia. Now I felt as if I'd received a shot in the arm. "Daddy, what are you smiling about?" Carol asked as she approached the couch with the shampoo I'd purchased in her hand.

"I have a lot to smile about," I answered, still smiling.

"Sometimes you can be so lame," she accused, shaking her head.

"So, you gave Regina a ride home, huh? I hope she doesn't pay us another unexpected visit again anytime soon," Marva said, dropping down next to me.

"Like last Monday when she just happened to be in our neighborhood just as we were about to have dinner. She's a nice lady and I like her, but I didn't like the way she manipulated an invitation from you to eat dinner with us that day," Carol added, sitting down on my other side. "Besides, you two don't even make a good couple."

"Carol, how would you know what it takes to make a couple good?" I asked as I gave her a playful tap on the side of her head.

"For one thing, when that lady is around, you look like you can't wait for her to leave."

"Pffftt! That's just your imagination," I suggested with a dismissive wave. "I've been friends with 'that lady' since we were in high school." I didn't know what to say next on the subject of Regina so I took a detour. "Let's pop some of that popcorn and go watch a movie. What do you queens want to watch tonight? *How the Grinch Stole Christmas* is coming on in a little while on channel two. Or we can check out that *Cinderella* movie your grandmother added to your video library the last time she visited."

"Daddy, please. We've seen so many versions of *Cinderella*. How about something from your library like the latest *Fast and Furious?*" Marva hollered.

"Okay. But only after I edit it first. That's too much action for girls your ages to watch."

They heaved out loud sighs at the same time. "For real, Daddy. You'll never find another wife being so straitlaced and dull," Marva predicted.

I shrugged and heaved out a loud sigh myself. "Well, queens, I guess I'll have to marry a straitlaced, dull woman."

CHAPTER 3
FELICIA

I had planned to pick up some Chinese takeout on my way home. But because of my clumsy encounter with Richard, I'd lost my appetite. I couldn't understand why running into him had me so flustered. I had known the man for over eight years! What was different about tonight was seeing the way Regina looked at him.

My two-bedroom, second-floor apartment was in a newly renovated three-story building on a quiet, tree-lined street next door to a barbershop. My landlady, a slim, attractive blonde named Lorena Jones, lived in the unit across the hall from mine. She was in her late thirties and divorced. Her elderly uncle, who lived in a re-

tirement home, owned the building. She managed it and got to live rent free. She and I had
become quite close since I'd moved in twelve
years ago.

I wasn't ready to go home so I knocked on
Lorena's door. She greeted me with a large glass
of tea in her hand. "Come on in, Fel. I was bored
so I wouldn't mind having some company." She
raked her long fingers through her hair and
waved me into her neatly organized living room.
"I didn't hear you go out," she continued, looking at the bag in my hand. Then she gazed at my
face and shook her head. "Baby, you don't look
too happy. Did something happen?"

"I'm fine," I muttered as we flopped down
onto her couch. "I . . . I saw a man that I have
feelings for with another woman at the market."

"Oh? Pam Williams's son? I didn't think you
and him were serious enough for you to get
upset over seeing him with another woman."

I waved my hand. "Pfffft! Puh-leeze! Clyde and
I are only friends and that's all we'll ever be."

Lorena took a sip of her tea and then waved
the glass in front of my face. "I have something
stronger than tea if you need a drink."

"No, thanks, I'm fine. I was going to pick up
some wine, but I was so anxious to get out of
Ralph's Market I forgot."

"If you change your mind let me know." Lorena took a deep breath and gave me a serious look. "Well, if it wasn't Clyde, who was it?"

"That's not important."

"It must be if it bothered you to see him with another woman. Are they in a serious relationship?"

"He has a lot of female friends, but I have no idea if he's in a serious relationship. That's one of the few things he's very vague about when I talk to him. Anyway, I've been admiring him from afar for years." Lorena and I shared a lot of personal information. However, I couldn't bring myself to tell her the identity of the man in question. She'd met Richard before so I couldn't even tell her what he looked like or where he worked. If I told her, she'd figure things out. As much as I adored Lorena, she had a long, busy tongue. My business would be all over the building in no time. By the time the story had made its rounds, it would have been embellished so much I'd come out looking like a love-struck fool. "The other woman, who looks like a supermodel all the time, was dressed to kill. And you see what I went out looking like."

Lorena looked me over and frowned. "You do look a little scraggly."

"If that wasn't bad enough, you should have

seen the way they stared at the things I bought."
I dumped my purchases onto the coffee table.

"I can see why." Lorena reared back and guffawed so hard, her eyes watered.

I kept talking and she kept laughing. "Except
for the Cheetos, this is all for Grandma Lucy.
But I have a feeling that they—at least the
woman—thinks these are items I bought for myself. I felt so old standing there."

Lorena got quiet and gave me a sympathetic
look. She set her glass on the end table and let
out a mighty belch. "Now, *that* made me feel
old," she complained as she rubbed her chest
and wiped her lips with the back of her hand. "I
was about to say, you don't have to feel old, or
any other way. Buy what you want and let people
think what they want. It's your life."

I put my merchandise back in the bag. "I better get on home. I forgot to take my phone with
me and I'm sure my grandmother has left me a
ton of voice mail messages."

"How long do you plan on pining for this fellow 'from afar'?"

I shrugged. "Lorena, I feel so silly talking
about this."

"Listen, there is nothing 'silly' about being in
love. Now answer the question I just asked."

"Well, I have a feeling that I'm probably as

close to him as I'll ever be," I whimpered. "I know he likes me, too—but his feelings are strictly platonic. He values my opinions, though. He's always complimenting me on my outfits and jewelry. He even asked me to go with him to Wallace Jewelers to help him pick out a birthday gift for his daughter and a Mother's Day gift for his mother-in-law this year."

Lorena gasped. "He's *married*?"

"Oh no! He's a widower, but he's still close to his former in-laws."

"Oh. If he still gives gifts to his former mother-in-law, he must be a keeper. After my divorce, my ex never spoke to my folks again, or me, for that matter. And, I have to admit, you do have good taste. I'd give an arm and a leg to own pieces of jewelry as sharp as some of the ones you own."

I tapped the pearl earrings in my ears I'd purchased last month. "Well, you know you can borrow anything you want from me." I exhaled, stretched my arms, and we stood up. "Thanks for listening to my woe-is-me rant again."

"Anytime. You know I'm always here for you."

"I'll see you tomorrow."

Lorena escorted me to the door and gave me a hug. "Fel, there are way too many other men on this planet for a woman to get the blues over one. Especially a woman with as much going for her as you. Besides, you still get a lot of attention from men. Maybe not from the ones you want, but the right guy will come your way eventually."

"I know. I'm just being silly and immature, I guess."

I was glad to be back in my cozy little apartment. My living room was large. But my computer station, a beige couch, matching love seat, two wing chairs, and a sixty-inch flat-screen TV made it look smaller. I had spent a lot of time and money on the pastel-colored curtains, oil paintings, and various knickknacks in every room.

When I changed out of my shabby attire, my appetite returned. Since I had not picked up the Chinese takeout, my supper was a turkey leg, a bowl of green beans, some dressing, and a Diet Coke. I watched a rerun of *Law & Order*, read a few pages of the most recent *Ebony* magazine, and took a hot bath. When my grandmother wasn't with me, I called her at least once or twice a day at her apartment to make sure she was doing okay. And to see if she needed anything. After my second call to her this morning, she'd called me back an hour later and given me a list of things to go pick up for her.

Grandma Lucy was an amazing woman. She

and my grandfather had dropped out of elementary school so they could go to work and help their folks pay bills. From that point on, they'd worked their fingers to the bone doing up to three jobs at a time each, sometimes six or seven days a week. They got married in their teens and started having babies right away, so they had to work even harder to support five children and pay for Mama to attend nursing school. My grandparents had been raised in Toxey, Alabama, a backwoods town with one stoplight and dirt roads, and they had moved to Ohio over sixty years ago. Grandma Lucy still spoke and acted like some of our relatives who still lived in the rural South. She had stopped driving and sold her car last month after she knocked over a mailbox, sideswiped a parked car, and almost skidded into a duck pond. There had been a few other incidents before that day, including several speeding tickets. I didn't want her to hurt anybody or herself, so I volunteered to chauffeur her around in my two-year-old Jetta.

"Gal, where my stuff at?" was how she greeted me when I called her up after I'd eaten.

"I got lazy so I'll bring it to you tomorrow morning."

"I'm going to the casino with my quilt-making club tomorrow and I'll be gone all day."

I cleared my throat. "Then I'll bring it to you on Sunday when I pick you up for church. Is everything okay?"

"Well, if it wasn't, I would have let you know by now," Grandma Lucy said with a chuckle. "You, your mama, and your daddy—and everybody else—worry too much about me. I been taking care of myself all these years and ain't had no problems yet. Stop treating me like a baby."

"Okay, sweetie."

"You sound tired, so why don't you get some rest. I'm fixing to go watch one of my Tyler Perry DVDs."

"I'll call you tomorrow."

"Girl, you done gone deaf? Didn't I just tell you I'll be gone all day tomorrow?"

"I was going to call you on the cellphone I bought you last month."

Grandma Lucy coughed and then said in a raspy tone, "I declare, I don't know why you bought me such a complicated contraption. And I ain't carrying it with me to the casino so it can be ringing and vibrating and distracting my attention away from them slot machines. I know you showed me how to use it, but I still can't figure it out. I been old school all my life and I'm going to stay that way." Old school was right. My grandmother was the only person I knew who still used a rotary telephone. She snorted and went on, "Every time I look up, they coming out with a new this, a new that. Especially that Internet. Faceback, Googly, chit rooms, and so on! All them strange words is enough to drive anybody nuts." She laughed some more. "And you expect me to learn how to use a phone that ain't even got no cord?"

"Well, when that rotary phone conks out, you'll have to get a *real* telephone."

"I ain't worried about that as long as what I got works for me. Shoot. My daddy told me all my life that if something wasn't broke, don't fix it."

"You are so bad," I teased. "Go watch your movie and don't forget to lock your door and take all your pills before you go to bed."

It had been a long day, so I went to bed an hour after my conversation with my grandmother and dozed off right away.

My brother, Victor, who was two years younger than me, lived in Atlanta with his wife and son. He was a very successful private investigator, and he was always on the go. But we kept in touch by video chatting, text, e-mail, and telephone at least three or four times a month. He had called me up on Thanksgiving Day, and we had chatted for almost a whole hour.

I never turned off my cellphone or my landline when I went to bed. With my elderly parents on a six-month-long vacation visiting cities in several countries, and a grandmother who lived alone in an apartment six blocks away, I wanted to be available at all times in case they needed to get in touch with me.

When my cellphone woke me up, I glanced at the illuminated clock on my nightstand and panicked. It was four a.m. "Oh, God," I moaned, sitting bolt upright. "Please let it be a wrong number." I swallowed hard and looked at the caller ID and saw a name and number I didn't recognize. I answered right away.

"Fel, were you asleep?" It was Mama's voice.

"I was," I muttered, and held my breath. "Is everything okay? Where's Daddy and whose phone are you using?"

"Everything's fine. We're having a ball down here in South Africa. Your daddy is flopping around in the hotel pool, and I'm stretched out on a chaise longue laughing at him and munching on a few things I took from the breakfast buffet. I left my phone in the room so I'm using one that belongs to a lady we met at breakfast this morning."

My parents had retired ten months ago on the same day. Mama had worked as a pediatric nurse for thirty-five years, and Daddy had worked in law enforcement for forty. He'd started out as a beat cop and worked his way up to homicide detective. One of their goals was to visit as many countries as possible before they got too old. Even after providing a good life for my brother and me, and supporting Daddy's parents until they passed years ago, they still managed to save enough money to fulfill their dream. A week before they were scheduled to begin their six-month-long vacation, Mama's father passed away and they didn't want to leave Grandma Lucy on her own. But she was in good health and didn't want them to change their plans to accommodate her. I didn't want them to change their plans either, so I assured them that I would take care of my grandmother and even suggested moving her in with me. Grandma Lucy liked living alone, but I picked her up at least once a week and brought her to my place to spend a couple of nights. Lorena enjoyed spending time with her while I was at work. And she wore a medic alert bracelet at all times when she was alone, so I wasn't too worried about her.

"How are you doing, baby? Is Mama driving you crazy yet?"

"I'm fine and so is she. She's going to spend today at a casino with one of her quilt-making club friends, but I'll see her on Sunday. How's the vacation going? It'll be over soon, so I hope you and Daddy are still having a good time."

They'd started their journey back in June and had already visited England, France, Scotland, Portugal, Ireland, and Italy. They had been in Africa for three weeks.

"Baby, we are having the time of our lives. Ghana was an amazing place, but we're enjoying Johannesburg, South Africa, even more. The people here, black and white, are so nice and friendly."

"So I've heard. That's one country I definitely plan to visit someday."

"Your daddy is a mess," Mama laughed. "We've been eating some tasty food, but he's disappointed because with all these black folks down here, we haven't found any restaurants that sell turnip greens, hush puppies, and smothered chicken. You know how addicted he is to soul food."

"Tell him he'll have to wait until he gets back to the States. Black folks in other countries have probably never even heard of what we call soul food."

"Tell me about it. But we've eaten some good food anyway. By the way, I spoke to your brother yesterday."

"I talked to him on Thanksgiving. He won't be able to make it up here for Christmas."

"That's another thing I need to tell you. We might not make it back in time for Christmas."

"Oh? Why not? We've always spent Christmas Day together."

"Our travel agent is working on getting us to the one place I never thought I'd get to visit." Mama paused and I held my breath until she continued. "If he can get us into a decent hotel, we'll spend Christmas Day and the rest of the week—if possible—in *Bethlehem.* A tour guide will take us to some of the same places where Jesus lived and preached. But our travel agent is having a few problems making the arrangements, so we're not going to get our hopes up too high."

I gasped. "Oh my. I hope he can get it done. When I was a little girl, you talked about visiting that part of the world all the time."

"If we do make it, I will call you on the Lord's birthday from His birthplace. Oooh wee. I get chills just thinking about being in the Holy Land. I just wanted to let you know now in case we don't make it back in time to spend Christmas Day at home. I hope you understand."

"Mama, don't worry about not making it back in time. If Grandma Lucy and I don't feel like cooking, I'm sure she'll want to eat Christmas dinner at Denny's. If we don't go there, we'll probably eat with my friend Pam and her family. So don't worry about us."

"I do worry about you being alone so much, though. . . ."

"Mama, I have my job and a lot of friends. And when I am alone, it doesn't bother me."

"Your grandma told your daddy that the only thing left on her bucket list is you getting married."

"It's not the *only* thing left on my list, but it's at the top," I giggled.

CHAPTER 4
RICHARD

Family was so important to me. I doted on my two precious daughters. My parents had passed four years ago in a fatal car crash and we'd always been very close. My older brother, Alex, lived in Jamaica with his wife and their three daughters. They were expecting their fourth child any day now. My sister-in-law had been on bed rest for four months, and her doctor had told her that she'd have to take it easy for at least six weeks after the baby came. That was the reason they wouldn't be coming home for Christmas.

I had several relatives in Ohio, and I spent as much time with them as possible. I still had a close relationship with my in-laws, too. When Margaret passed, her mother and mine both offered to move in with me and help raise my girls. I knew a lot of folks who had been raised by grandmothers, but there was no reason I couldn't raise my own children. Besides, it was time for black grandmothers to stop being so overburdened. Most of the ones I knew had already done more than enough for their children, grandchildren, and in a lot of cases, great-grandchildren.

I had decided that if any other woman was going to live with me and help raise my children, she and I would have to be married.

No woman could replace my beloved Margaret. But I knew that there were other women just as phenomenal as she had been. However, finding one I liked and getting her to fall in love with me enough to make a long-term commitment was not easy. Even though I had been involved with several ladies since Margaret's passing, Felicia was the only one who had grabbed my attention and kept it. At first it was just as a friend. She was caring, generous, sensitive, funny, smart, and very easy on the eyes. Each time I was in her presence, I felt my feelings for her grow.

Raising two teenagers was no picnic. After Margaret died, almost everybody I knew started warning me with comments like, "Man, when they get in their teens, you're going to have a mess on your hands." One well-meaning cousin told me, "They'll end up running the show and you won't know what hit you." Other than a few issues about cellphone use, the TV shows they watched, music choices, and their spending too much time on their computers, I hadn't experienced anything to be too concerned about yet. I gave my kids everything they needed, including a fair amount of freedom. But my tolerance level for bad behavior was zero. When they started paying more attention to their phones than to me and their dinner, I stopped allowing them to bring their phones to the table. To make sure they were not doing anything dangerous or inappropriate online, I checked their computers and phones on a daily basis. They didn't like that at all. "And don't even think about deleting things you don't want me to see," I warned. "Deleted only means relocated." Thanks to one of the courses I had taken advantage of in the army, I probably knew as much about electronics as the people who invented them.

Saturday was the girls' favorite day in the week because I let them sleep in as long as they wanted, and I didn't check to see what they were up to in their rooms. But I wasn't naïve. There was just no telling what kind of mischief they got into when they were on their own and when I let them sleep over at their friends' houses. I wasn't too worried about them associating with a bad crowd because I monitored that as much as I could. Even though I knew their friends and their parents, it was impossible to keep track of every move they made. I had done a lot of stupid things when I was a kid—some my parents never knew about—but I'd learned from my mistakes.

I tumbled out of bed right after daybreak this morning. I planned to go out early and fill up my gas tank, run a few errands, and come home and relax. I had gone to bed last night with a lot of thoughts bouncing around in my head. I was having a transmission problem with my Ford Explorer and needed to get it taken care of soon. That would be a major expense, and it couldn't have come at a worse time, because my Christmas gift list was two pages long. The cost of buying presents for so many people each year, including my girls, always set me back a pretty penny. But because of my careful spending habits and some good investments, I had a pretty sweet nest egg to fall back on.

Marva and Carol had been badgering me for months to let them start wearing makeup and get their nails done. I'd finally proposed a compromise last night after we'd watched *Spider-Man: Homecoming* for the third time since its release last year. "A little lip gloss and manicures with clear polish," I told them.

"I want a French manicure," Carol whined. "Clear polish is only for old women in their twenties and thirties."

"Clear polish," I insisted.

"What about boys?" Marva brought up in a meek tone.

"What about boys?" I echoed, giving her a stern what's-wrong-with-you-girl look.

"James Noah asked me to go to the movies with him this coming weekend. Can I go?"

"I'll have to check and see if I'm available to go that day," I said.

"Daddy, you can't go on a date with me and a boy," she protested.

"You can't either. We've discussed this subject before, and more than once. No dating until you're sixteen. You can have boys for friends, they can continue to come to the house to watch movies and play video games *when I'm home* or if some other adult is here. I don't think it's a good idea for girls your ages to be out on a bus with a boy going to the movies."

"James is sixteen and his daddy lets him borrow his car all the time," Marva tossed in with a major pout.

"Well, when you turn sixteen, you can ride with James," I said, keeping my voice gentle.

"Girl, I told you," Carol said under her breath.

My girls didn't sulk often or for too long. Half an hour later, we popped more corn and I played a couple of video games with them before they went to bed.

After I took a quick shower, I checked on the girls. They were still asleep and still clutching their cellphones. I sighed and shook my head and crept quietly out of the house.

My Explorer still had half a tank of gas, so I didn't have to go to the gas station today after all. But there was one other thing I had to attend to. Other than my late wife's parents, I was probably the only person who remembered that today was the day Margaret died. On the first anniversary, the girls went to the cemetery with me to put fresh flowers on her grave. But they'd cried off and on the rest of that day, so I never took them again. I had not missed a year yet.

Ralph's Market had poinsettias already, so I stopped there first and purchased one of the biggest pots they had. After a cup of coffee and a muffin at a nearby coffee shop, I drove to the Mandell Cemetery, which was located on the outskirts of town. I parked on the side of the road and dragged my feet to Margaret's grave. I had forgotten to put on my gloves, so when I brushed the snow off her headstone, the cold chill felt like needles pricking my fingers. "Sure do miss you," I whispered. I stared at her name and the dates of her sunrise and sunset. When I kissed the top of her headstone, I didn't even feel the cold. As a matter of fact, I felt warm all over.

When I got back home, the girls were in the kitchen making breakfast. "Where have you been, Daddy?" Marva demanded. She stood over the stove scrambling what looked like half a dozen eggs in the frying pan. Carol immediately poured me a cup of coffee from the pot she'd just made.

"I went to visit Mommy." I swallowed hard and closed my eyes for a few seconds. "I hope she's warm." I immediately wished I could take back my last comment.

"She is warm, Daddy. Everybody knows that the weather and everything else in heaven is perfect," Marva said, choking on a sob.

"Did you take her some flowers?" Carol asked as she set my cup on the table. Her tone was shaky and just above a whisper. "Mama loved flowers."

"I took her some," I replied in the most cheerful tone I could manage. I removed my coat and draped it on the back of the chair I usually occupied. And then I plopped down and took a sip of my coffee.

Carol sat down across from me. "Daddy, you don't have to keep going out there by yourself. We can start going with you again," she said with a sniffle.

"We miss Mama as much as you do. We're older now and we don't get sad like we did that first time we went with you," Marva added.

"Okay, queens," I said, puffing out my chest. Marva plopped down on the seat next to her sister. The weary looks on their faces bothered me, and now I wished I had not told them I'd been to the cemetery. It was time for me to lighten the mood since I was the one who had darkened it. I looked toward the stove and sniffed. "Let's dig into those eggs before they get cold."

CHAPTER 5
FELICIA

Shortly after I got out of bed Saturday morning, I decided to call up a few elderly members who belonged to my church to see if they wanted any assistance this weekend. These people had outlived most of their family and friends. Even though they needed help from time to time, they had no desire to check into nursing homes. Mama had been helping them out ever since I could remember. But because she was busy fulfilling her dream to travel, I volunteered my free services two or three times a month. This was a very important and honorable role to me. I planned to do it as long as I could. Since there was a strong possibility that

I'd never have children to assist me in my old age, I hoped that somebody would help look out for me when the time came. I left messages for the first three. I told each one to call me if they needed my help in any way. My last call was to ninety-three-year-old Mervis Wheeler, one of Grandma Lucy's posse. "Fel, you are so sweet to think of me. I thank God every time I hear from you. You're as devoted as your mama. But I don't need anything right now. My grandson is on his way up from Kentucky to bring me down there for Christmas."

"Okay, Sister Mervis. When you return, let me know if you need anything."

"I will, sugar. You've done so much for me these past few months, I wish I could do something for you." There was a brief pause before Mervis continued. "God is going to bless you."

"He already has. I have everything I need." *Everything except Richard and children of my own.* I was glad I had such a busy life. However, there were times when all I wanted to do was relax, read a good book, and watch TV. That was what I planned to do today. After two cups of coffee and a light breakfast, I made a beeline for my living-room couch.

Before I could get comfortable, somebody knocked on my door. I assumed it was Lorena. I peered through the peephole and saw a huge eye looking back at me. I cracked the door open, but left the security chain in place. "Clyde? What are you doing here?" I glanced at my watch and added, "At eight fifteen a.m."

"Fel, I'm in a jam. Can I come in and use your phone? I just ran out of gas and I didn't bring my cellphone with me," he wailed.

Clyde Williams was the forty-year-old, divorced, unemployed son of Pam Williams, one of my senior coworkers and a close friend. His divorce last year had been very bitter and now he suffered bouts of depression. We used to belong to the same bowling team until six months ago when they closed the alley for renovations. One evening three months ago I visited Pam while Clyde was there. He was moping around with a long face because a woman he'd been seeing for two months had abruptly ended their relationship. Pam suggested I go to the movies with him to help bring him out of the doldrums. I'd reluctantly gone, and had been going out with him several times a month ever since. He was not classically handsome, but he wasn't a bad-looking man. His piercing black eyes and smooth caramel-colored skin were his best features, but he could stand to lose a few pounds off his five-foot-six-inch frame. He had never shown any romantic interest in me, and it was just as well. That was not something I wanted with him. But there were other benefits. We had several things in common. Pizza topped with bacon, hot sauce on collard greens, and Snapple were just a few. He was the only man I knew who didn't laugh or tease me when he found out how many Godzilla DVDs I had in my video library.

"Sure, you can come in," I said as I motioned for him to enter my living room. Clyde had on a heavy coat but no earmuffs or gloves. His ears and hands were beet-red. "Have a seat and I'll get you a cup of coffee to help warm you up."

"No, that's okay." He paused and blew on his hands. "I was on my way home from a date. I met this woman at the mall last Monday. She invited me to her house last night and I took her to dinner. It was so late when we got back, she told me I could stay the night if I didn't mind sleeping on her couch."

I padded across the floor, grabbed my cellphone off the coffee table, and handed it to him. "Well, I hope you had a good time."

"I did, but I won't be seeing her again too soon. At the restaurant, she ordered steak and lobster and then had the nerve to order the same thing to go—to take to the teenage son she had forgot to mention until last night. Right after he gobbled up that food, he asked to use my truck. I hesitated, but his mama made a big fuss about it just 'sitting in the driveway,' so I gave him the key. I don't know where he went, and when I woke up this morning, I was so anxious to leave, I didn't think to check my gas. I'm lucky I made it as far as your street."

"Where is your truck now?"

"Parked at the end of this block." Clyde pulled out his wallet. "Oh, shoot! I forgot my Triple A card—"

"Don't worry. I can take you to get gas. Let me make you some breakfast first, though. And some hot coffee."

"Oh, all right then." He paused and gave me a pensive look. "Fel, sometimes I don't know what I'd do without you. I tell my mama all the time, you must be the best lady friend I got. I can't figure out why you ain't married."

I didn't even respond to Clyde's last comment.

After breakfast, I drove him to a gas station and promised to go to the movies with him next week.

I had a key to my grandmother's apartment, so I let myself in Sunday morning a few minutes before eight a.m. "Yoo-hoo, I'm here!" I yelled. I glanced around the living room. I shook my head and chuckled. Grandma Lucy was a borderline hoarder. She had useless knickknacks all over her two-bedroom apartment. One was a *spodik*, a tall fur hat worn by some Hasidic Jews. It sat on top of a defunct VHS VCR player she had purchased only because it had been marked down to a dollar. It didn't matter that the thing no longer worked or that we didn't know anybody who still owned VHS tapes. "Grandma Lucy, you home?" I yelled louder, looking around some more. Just as I was about to panic, she stumbled into the living room, dressed in one of her boxy beige pantsuits, mismatched jewelry, and a black turban.

"I ain't deaf. So you ain't got to holler like that," she scolded as she walked toward me holding her coat and purse. "It took you long enough to get here. I was beginning to think you'd forgot we were going shopping today."

"Shopping? I thought we were going to church."

"Pffftt!" She gave me a dismissive wave. "Church, schmurch! If all the time I done already spent in church for almost ninety years don't get me into heaven, nothing will." Grandma Lucy gave me an apologetic look and then a tight smile. "Now I hope that didn't sound too disrespectful or blasphemous. You know I love the Lord, but I like to lighten things up from time to time. It's boring being too holy and walking too straight and narrow. Shoot. I need to have some worldly fun every now and then. God even said ain't none of us perfect—except Jesus—so I know he expects us to stray now and then. Besides, I'm donating half of the four hundred and forty dollars I won yesterday at the casino to the soup kitchen."

"I'm sure the soup kitchen will appreciate your generosity, Grandma Lucy." I gave her a hug and tickled her chin. "The stores you like won't be open for another hour, so we can go eat breakfast first."

"Good. Take me to someplace real swanky."

"You mean like that seafood place where Mayor Gibson and other celebrities eat?"

"I mean like IHOP."

After breakfast, we meandered around for the next eight hours and picked up everything from turnip roots at a farmer's market to a set of wooden spoons at Goodwill. On the way home, Grandma Lucy suddenly ordered me to drive to the south side to a thrift shop one of her friends had told her about. She didn't have the address, the name of the place, or the phone number of the person who had told her about it, so that part of the trip was a waste of time. I never complained about all the roaming around we did, but it made my grandmother feel badly. "I am so sorry I wasted up so much of your time, sweetie."

"I don't look at it that way. Every minute I spend with you is important to me. I don't care how many times we go on a wild goose chase. I can't think of anybody else I'd rather 'waste' my time on."

From the endearing look on my grand-mother's face as we cruised toward the freeway, I could tell my words meant a lot to her. And I meant every one of them. No matter how many times she "complained" about wasting my time, I never complained. "I'd spend even more time with you if I didn't have to work," I assured her.

"You're such a good girl. You need to be doing things other women your age are doing, like raising a family. When are you going to get married? I can't wait to see that happen. It's the last thing on my bucket list."

"So I've heard. . . ."

"Fel, don't you have at least one special friend?"

"Yes. But I don't want to discuss him until I know where our relationship is going."

"I understand, sugar. He's shy, huh?"

"Something like that."

Grandma Lucy chuckled. "Your granddaddy was too. Shy men make the best husbands be-cause they are too timid to argue. I hope your special friend ain't too shy to propose to you someday—if he's the one. Whether he is or not,

I promise you I ain't going to leave this earth until you get a husband."

"Then you might live a whole lot longer than you think," I teased. "Do you want to come spend the night with me?"

"Naw. Baby, you are so good to me, but I don't want to wear you out. I done took up enough of your time today. Now take me to my apartment before I miss *Judge Judy*."

When I got home, I stepped out of my shoes and dropped down onto my couch. Just as I was about to call up Pam, her caller ID popped up on my cellphone screen. "Hey, girl. How was church today?" she asked.

"I didn't go. Grandma Lucy wanted to go shopping instead."

"Oh. I just wanted to thank you for taking Clyde to get gas this morning. My baby told me about his bad date with some woman that picked him up at the mall. Tsk, tsk, tsk."

"Yeah. Well, I don't think you have to worry about him getting too close to her."

"You want me to send him back over there to take you to the movies or out to eat this evening?"

I took my time answering. "No, that's okay. We're going to the movies next week, if he's available." I swallowed hard and took a deep breath so I could get the next sentence out without stuttering. "Um, Pam, I ran into Richard Friday evening at Ralph's Market."

"So?"

"He was with Regina."

"So?" Pam repeated. "I see him with her a lot. What's it to you?"

"Nothing, really. It's just that I was looking a hot mess. I didn't have on any makeup. I had a do-rag on my head and boots even my grandmother makes fun of."

"Fel, you're one of the prettiest women I know, with or without makeup. You could never look a 'hot mess' in my book—even when you look a hot mess."

"But Regina *always* looks perfect."

"Well, I can't argue with that. And she's a nice person. That's something I can't say about most of the good-looking women I know. I wouldn't be surprised if she and Richard end up getting married one day after all."

"What? What do you mean by 'after all'?"

"Didn't you know? I guess you didn't mingle with her crowd in high school. Anyway, Clyde was in some of the same classes with Richard and Regina. They were real hot and heavy back then. They got even more serious in college. Everybody expected them to get married someday. But right after they graduated, he joined the army and she married another man while he was overseas."

"I didn't know that. I knew she was divorced and has been friends with Richard for years. But I never knew they'd once been in a serious relationship."

"Humph. Between her and some of those flirtatious females at the office, I'm surprised Richard hasn't remarried. He's such a good catch. I never knew a man so devoted to his children. His mama sure raised him right. He'll make a good husband, if he ever decides to remarry. Won't he?"

"Yeah. He will."

CHAPTER 6
RICHARD

"Daddy, can I get a nose ring?" Carol asked while we were eating breakfast Monday morning.

"Now, you know better," I snapped. A split second later, I gave her a smile. "If I let you do that, next thing I know you'll want a tattoo."

"Marsha Lawson just got a tattoo of a cute dragon on her leg," Marva zoomed in.

I loved our early-morning chats, whether they were pleasant or not. Most of the time they were. Despite my strictness, sometimes I weakened and let them have their way. But I was determined to be firm today. "Tattoos are absolutely out of the question. When I was a teenager, the only people I knew with tattoos were criminals, bikers, and circus freaks," I said. "And guys in the military," I added with a sheepish grin. I tossed that in before they had time to make a remark about the rose tattoo on my right bicep.

"We can't wear real makeup yet, go on dates with boys unless you go with us, stay up too late, hang out with certain kids, and you monitor our phones and computers, and what we watch on TV," Carol complained. "Some kids can do whatever they want."

"Not *my* kids!" I boomed. I softened my response with a wide smile and some practical advice. "It's safer and smarter to stay within your boundaries."

"Like you would let us get out of our boundaries," Carol scoffed.

"Exactly," I fired back, looking from one face to the other and gently wagging my finger. Marva snickered first and then Carol joined her. "All right now." I clapped my hands and rose from the table. "Finish up, go wash your faces and hands, and grab your backpacks so we can be on our way. I don't want to miss my bus."

I loved living in Mandell, Ohio. It was a nice, quiet suburb of Cleveland with a very low crime rate. And it was a great place to raise children. Public transportation was very convenient, and I took advantage of it when I didn't feel like driving. Webb Street Middle School was only four blocks from the four-bedroom house my late mother had inherited from her grandparents and left to me in her will. Rather than share ownership of the house with me, my brother had preferred the generous insurance policy our parents had left. He'd used the money to buy a beach house in Montego Bay, Jamaica, and start a dive shop business, which had done so well in the first six months, he'd opened two more a year later. My neighborhood had a vigilant crime-watch team, and our police department was less than a mile away, so I didn't have to worry about my girls walking to and from school. But whenever I decided to drive to work, I always offered to drop them off in front of their school first.

"Ooh, I forgot! I didn't finish my math assignment," Marva wailed.

"And why didn't you? You started working on it right after dinner last night."

"Um, my laptop screen froze and the next thing I knew—*babam*! I was so sleepy I couldn't keep my eyes open. Daddy, can you fix my computer? If I don't turn it in, Mrs. Brown will fuss at me in front of the whole class."

I groaned. "That excuse is not good enough. I will fix your problem and make sure you get your homework done before I leave. Starting today, you'll both finish your homework *before* you eat dinner so I can make sure it gets done on time. And until it's done to my satisfaction each evening, I'll hold on to your cellphones."

"Dang," Carol muttered under her breath.

"All our friends can use their phones anytime they want to," she pointed out.

"If they lived under my roof, they wouldn't. They'd follow my rules, or find another place to live," I said with a smile. But the girls knew that I always meant what I said, so they never pushed too hard. "Do I make myself clear?"

"Yes, Daddy," they said at the same time.

Unfreezing Marva's screen took only a couple of minutes. She had completed only half of her assignment, but I made her finish it and that took another twenty minutes. So that they wouldn't be too late, I decided to drive them to school. By the time I did that, it was too late for me to catch my regular bus, so I decided to drive to the office.

Some people worked to live. I loved my job so much, I lived to work. Training and Management Development was a great company to work for. Our highly skilled trainers, twelve the last time I counted, facilitated workshops that helped management employees hone their skills, improve interpersonal relationships, and develop any other area in which they needed improvement. Each year we received at least an eight-stars-out-of-ten rating score for our classes. Our company even produced training videos. Two hundred full-time permanent employees and several temps occupied the second and third floors of an eighteen-floor office building only a couple of miles from downtown Cleveland. We had a smaller office in Louisville, Kentucky, and our home office was in Indianapolis, Indiana. A lot of external companies sent employees to attend our classes, so all three locations were busy most of the year.

The pay and benefits were spectacular. Most of my coworkers were nice people and easy to work with. Another perk was that I didn't have to wear a suit and tie every day. I could wear jeans and a pullover sweater, or other casual attire whenever I wanted. I did suit up when I knew honchos from the home office were going to be on the premises, and when we had special celebrations.

Some of our classes lasted only two or three days, but most of them were five days long. Equipment was always breaking down, so the company put my electronic skills to good use. Some days I had so many repair requests, I had to come in early and stay late to complete them all. I supervised four other technical support employees. The five of us also fulfilled the reprographic and photocopy issues.

I had a small office with a view of a brick wall on the third floor at the end of the hall a few steps from the elevators. The other technicians occupied individual cubicles across from my office. Our manager, Sam Morello, had a huge office at the other end of the hall. He had a great view of Lake Erie.

Felicia's office was directly below mine on the second floor. Every chance I got, I wandered down to her floor, hoping I'd see her.

CHAPTER 7
FELICIA

I was disappointed when I didn't see Richard on the bus this morning. He and Pam lived at one end of the route, so they were among the first people to get on each day. By the time I boarded, four stops later, most of the good seats were gone. But when Richard was on the bus, he'd save the seat right beside him for me. Pam always sat in the aisle seat directly across from us. We always sat near the back because it was quieter. Some commuters in the rear seats either slept or read for most of the twenty-five-minute ride. In the eight years we'd been following this routine, the three of us had become close. We discussed everything from our work to what was happening in the news. We socialized together on special occasions and always with some of our other coworkers and friends present. Each morning that we rode on the same bus, Pam dominated the conversation by talking about her personal life. But Richard and I only shared the basics. I knew he dated, but I didn't know how serious he was about anyone in particular. And vice versa.

Today when I got on the bus, Pam was in the spot Richard usually occupied, so I sat down next to her. Within seconds, she started yakking away about how wonderful her Thanksgiving dinner had been. I couldn't get a word in edgewise. She finished her monologue five minutes later with, "Girl, with my blood pressure, I don't need to be eating the way I do. What did you do after I talked to you last night?"

"Nothing special," I said with a shrug.

"Hmmm. Well, it could have been special if you had come to my house. You missed hearing the speech my grandson is going to recite at his school Christmas program. And I forgot to ask you if you went to some of the Black Friday sales."

I shook my head.

"Why not? Did you have company?" I shook my head again.

"Humph! That's a shame. You spend too

much time by yourself. I keep telling my son he needs to spend more time with you—"

"Pam, Clyde and I are just friends. You know that," I reminded. "He's more interested in other women anyway."

"Yeah, but you and my baby look so cute together," Pam said with misty eyes and a chuckle. She was the kind of upbeat, resourceful, and wise old sister you read about in old books and poems. And she was as stylish and attractive as a tubby, moon-faced woman in her sixties could be. She wore a purple tweed suit underneath her gray coat, and black boots that zipped in the front. As usual, her thick gray-and-black hair was neatly coiffed today. "You're so much smarter and prettier than some of the other women my baby spends time with. Oh well. His first wife was so unexciting. No wonder their marriage didn't work. If he ever gets married again, I hope it's with a ball of fire like you—even if it's not you."

"Well, this 'ball of fire' stopped blazing so long ago, marriage is probably not in my near future," I said in a detached voice.

Pam gasped. "Girl, you can have any man you want!"

"I don't know about that." I sighed. "That may have been true when I was younger. I dated a lot in high school and college. When I was twenty-two, two different men asked me to marry them.

But I wanted a career first. Poor Mama. She couldn't believe I turned down marriage proposals from two different men in the same year." I laughed. "She can't wait for me to marry and have children. I promised her years ago that when and if I ever accept a proposal, she'd be the first to know."

"That's one promise I hope you keep."

"I will." I bit my bottom lip and gave Pam a thoughtful look. I noticed another female commuter in the seat in front of us staring at me, so I lowered my voice. "Pam, can I tell you something?"

"You can tell me anything you want. Who is it about?" Her eyes got so big I thought they were going to pop out of her head. As nice and sweet as Pam was, she loved to hear gossip as much as she loved to share things she'd heard or suspected. Even with a husband, Clyde back in the house, and six other grown kids in and out of her house with their kids, she still had a lot of time on her hands. "Is it about somebody at work? I bet it's about Ramona, that clerk of yours who's going to marry that bartender." When Pam stopped talking, she tilted her head and gave me a pleading look. "Who is it you have something to tell me about? I'm usually the one with all the good news to report."

Before I answered, I took a deep breath and

looked around the bus. The woman who had been staring had dozed off and the few people I knew sat too many seats away to hear what I had to say. But I kept my voice low anyway. "It's about me."

By now, Pam was looking at me like she was about to drool. "What did *you* do?"

"I didn't do anything," I whimpered. "Maybe I shouldn't tell you. . . ."

"Shouldn't tell me what? Look, I am a patient woman, but don't you dare leave me with a cliff-hanger!" she barked.

I held my breath and looked at her with a puppy-dog expression on my face. The next thing I knew, the words tumbled out of my mouth before I could stop them. "I'm in love."

"Pffftt! Is that all?" Pam giggled. "I thought you had something to tell me that I could sink my teeth into. Are you in love with anybody I know?"

I had to force out the rest of my confession. "Richard."

Pam gave me a puzzled look. "Richard who? That cute security guard at Ralph's Market?"

"His name is Randy."

"Richard? Hmmm. I don't know but one other Richard in Mandell." She abruptly stopped talking and narrowed her eyes. "Do you mean—"

All I did was blink and nod. That told her all she needed to know.

Her eyes got as big as saucers and then it looked like her face had frozen solid. Several seconds passed before her lips thawed out enough for her to speak again. "Richard *Grimes*?"

I nodded again.

Pam's jaw dropped so low, I was surprised it didn't touch her chest. She gave me the most incredulous look anybody had ever given me. "Did I hear you right?"

"You heard right," I confirmed.

"Sweet Jesus, Felicia! When did this happen?"

Pam sounded frantic, but I kept my voice low and gentle. "I've always been fond of him."

"Always? Even before his wife passed?"

"Of course not. I only thought of him as a good friend back then. I didn't start feeling the way I feel now until about three years ago. No, it started before that. It was almost four years ago."

"And you waited this long to tell *me*?"

"I just got up enough nerve." I paused and gave Pam a pitiful look. "I'm glad I finally did. Being in love with somebody from afar can be such a burden. Now that I've told you, I feel better already."

"I'm glad you finally told me too. It's going to take me a while to digest a confession like that! Who else knows you're in love with Richard?"

"Just you. I told my landlady I was in love, but I didn't tell her who with. Those loose-lipped women at work would run something like this into the ground, so please don't tell them."

"I won't."

"Can you go to lunch with me today?"

"I don't know yet. There is so much work on my desk, I might have to work through lunch, or stay later the next couple of weeks to get caught up." The incredulous look was back on Pam's face. "I . . . just don't know what to say! You've been walking around acting normal when you have what we OGs used to call a love-jones—all this time."

"All this time," I confirmed.

"Have mercy," Pam mouthed. "If I can get one of the other secretaries to do a couple of projects for me, we can go for coffee later this morning, and you can tell me more about why you think you're in love with Richard."

"I don't 'think,' I know. I have never felt so strongly about a man. Not even the two who asked me to marry them."

"All these years the three of us have been working together and riding the same bus to and from work, and the man of your dreams was sitting within reach."

"Right beside me," I said.

CHAPTER 8
RICHARD

I had already warmed up my SUV and moved it from the garage to the driveway by the time the girls collected their backpacks and got into their coats, gloves, earmuffs, and boots. It had snowed quite a bit during the night and it was still coming down. I knew that by the time I got home, I'd have to do some serious shoveling. I didn't mind, though. A few years ago, Marva and Carol used to make snowmen while I shoveled and then we'd have snowball fights. Now they balked when I mentioned that, claiming, "Snowball fights and building snowmen are for little kids."

Before we could get out the door, the living-room landline on the end table rang. If I hadn't been close enough to see my former mother-in-law's name on the caller ID, I would have let the call go to voice mail. "Go get buckled in and let me take this call," I told the girls waving them out the door. I grabbed the phone on the third ring. "Hello, Mother Pritchard."

"Hello, son. I expected to get your voice mail. Aren't you going to work today?"

"Yes, I'm just running a little late. What's up?"

"I know you and the girls were just here for Thanksgiving last week, but Drew and I would love to have them spend at least a week of their two-week Christmas vacation with us. We'll even come pick them up."

"That sounds nice. But can I get back to you on that in a couple of days?"

"You're welcome to come if you can take a few days off work. You can even bring that woman you brought to the last Cavaliers game we attended. Gina was her name, right?"

"Regina," I corrected. I should have clarified that *she'd* taken me to the game with an extra ticket she just "happened to have." But it wasn't important enough to go into. It didn't matter how many times my in-laws encouraged me to remarry or meet other women, the subject made me uncomfortable. Especially when it involved Regina. As much as I enjoyed her company, there was no way I was going to invite her to spend Christmas with me and my family. If that didn't send the wrong message to her, nothing would. She had never actually said it, but I had a feeling she figured we'd eventually become more than just friends if she spent enough time with me. As long as I was hung up on Felicia that would never happen.

"The only thing is, if you bring her, she'll have to go outside when she wants to smoke."

"I'm sure Regina's already made plans for Christmas. She's a very busy lady. Thanks for inviting me, though. But I think I'll stay home. I'll check with the girls and see what they want to do. If they want to come, that's fine with me. I can throw together a meal for myself and watch one of the games I recorded." I chuckled.

A moment of silence passed before Mother Pritchard responded. "That's a shame. If Regina doesn't have time for you, you don't have another lady friend you can spend the holiday with? I don't like knowing you're sitting in that house by yourself watching TV and eating alone."

"Oh, I'm sure one of my buddies will drop by later in the day. Or, I might go visit one of them. Our favorite sports bar sells half-price beer after seven p.m. until they close at midnight on Christmas Day."

"Richard, we want you to be happy. We know

how much you loved our daughter, but she's gone. You'd be so much happier and even more well-rounded if you had a good woman to share your life with."

"I'm just fine. I don't need to share my life with a woman." Those words didn't even convince me. But the woman I wanted to share my life with was unreachable.

"That's the same thing my brother Wilbur said when his wife died. He almost drank himself to—"

I was glad one of the girls honked the horn. The timing was perfect. "Mother, I hate to cut you off, but the girls are getting restless. And I really do need to get them to school and myself to work."

"Okay, sugar. Let me know what they want to do as soon as you can."

By the time I got out the door, it had gotten even colder. A gust of icy-cold air hit my face so hard it almost took my breath away. I scrambled into my vehicle as fast as I could. Both girls occupied the front seat with Carol in the middle. "Who was that on the phone?" she asked, looking at me with her eyes narrowed.

"Your grandmother," I said as I started the motor.

"Daddy, don't you dare drive off until you put on your seat belt," Marva told me, wagging her finger in my face.

"Sorry." I immediately buckled up. "Grandma Pritchard wants to know if you two want to spend a week of your Christmas vacation in Cleveland."

"Nope," they said at the same time.

"We were just there last week for Thanksgiving," Carol added. "We still have tons of Christmas shopping to do. And you said we could go to that three-day party at the ice skating rink with our friends."

"Daddy, you promised," Marva whined. "And anyway, we always go to Grandma's house every year for New Year's Day."

"Okay, don't get too riled up about it. I'll let your granny know we'll all be up there for New Year's Day."

I barely made it to work on time. When I got a few feet from my office, I was surprised to see that my door was open. As I got closer, I could hear somebody inside grunting and mumbling under their breath. I assumed it was one of the other technicians. It was our executive manager, Sam Morello, pacing back and forth in front of my desk mopping sweat off his face with a white napkin. He was a high-strung dude who resembled a middle-aged Justin Bieber. But he was also very likable and well respected. He didn't micromanage and he was fair when it came to promoting people and passing out bonuses. Unfortunately, he was also a scatterbrain. He'd missed his granddaughter's First Communion this year because he'd shown up at the wrong church. He misplaced everything from his cellphone to his briefcase. He accidently threw away important documents on a regular basis, so several times a week I'd see him or his secretary rooting through the trash can in his office.

There was a frantic look on Sam's face. "Morning, Rich. My secretary called in sick and her files are a mess. I can't find anything! Do you still have that memo from the home office with a list of next year's classes?" he asked. "I need it for my presentation this afternoon."

"No problem." Before I removed my coat, I opened the top drawer in the file cabinet behind my desk, pulled out the memo in question, and handed it to him. "It's a copy, so you can keep it."

"Thanks!" Sam boomed as he mopped more sweat off his forehead. With a loud sigh of relief, he tossed the sweat-soaked napkin into my trash can. "You just saved me again. When you get time, put a new toner cartridge in my printer. And since Shirley is out and I don't know when she'll be back, please water my plants before you leave today. I know I'll forget to do that myself." I wore a lot of hats in my day-to-day life, so I didn't mind being my boss's temporary secretary from time to time.

Around ten a.m., after I'd made some adjustments on one of our heavy-duty copy machines, I decided to take a break. We had a break room on the third floor, which was where I usually went to have coffee a couple of times each day, especially when the weather was as nasty as it was today. But this time I decided to go to the cafeteria. It was located on the second floor, not far from Felicia's office. She and Pam were walking in my direction as I made my way to the elevator. They looked at each other and then at me, which made me suspect they'd been talking about me.

"Hello, ladies," I greeted.

"Good morning, Richard," Pam chirped.

"Hi, Richard," Felicia mumbled, and blinked rapidly a few times.

"We missed you on the bus this morning," Pam said with a curious look on her face. "Is everything okay?" She was the lead secretary in our personnel department, a few doors down the hall from my office. She had become a mother figure to a lot of our coworkers over the years, so everybody liked her. Two or three times a week, she brought sweets she'd baked and set them on the counter in the break room. She was nosy and slightly annoying at times, but the place was not the same when she wasn't on the premises. Nobody was looking forward to her upcoming retirement next year.

"Everything is fine," I answered. "I had something to take care of before I left the house, so I decided to drive in." From the corner of my eye, I noticed the blank look on Felicia's face as she gazed at me. I cleared my throat and turned to her. "Felicia, you can let your team know that we've already printed out the schedules for the December classes. They were a little concerned that they'd be late again."

"Thanks, Richard. I'm sure they'll be glad to hear that. I told them they could count on you."

Felicia shifted her weight from one foot to the other. She seemed almost as fidgety as she had been when I bumped into her Friday night at the market. I was glad Pam broke the silence. "Richard, if you don't have any plans for Christmas, you and your girls are welcome to come to my house." She paused, looked at Felicia, and added, "You can even bring a date."

"Thanks, Pam. I'll keep that in mind." I was glad when the elevator arrived. I held the door open. "You ladies going down?"

"No, you go on ahead. We're on our way to the break room," Pam blurted out. I saw her jab Felicia in the side before the door closed. Now I *knew* they'd been talking about me. And I couldn't imagine what they'd said.

CHAPTER 9
FELICIA

Pam never ceased to amaze me. When the elevator door closed completely, I glared at her. "What's the matter with you? You didn't have to go there."

"Didn't have to go where?"

"Tell Richard he could 'bring a date.'"

"Well, if you want to come to my house for Christmas, you can bring a date too."

"Don't hold your breath," I said with a sharp laugh. "And if you don't mind, let's not talk about Richard again today."

"That's fine with me. By the way, did you see the way he looked at you?" Pam asked with a sly gaze.

"He looked at me the same way he always looks at me."

"Exactly."

I threw up my hands and we continued walking toward the break room, passing office doors that had already been decorated with streamers and wreaths. I made a mental note to hang my wreath on my door when I returned to my office, and start looking for a tree in the next week or so. I always waited until the middle of December. But with my parents gone this year, I wanted to get more in the holiday mood sooner.

I knew that if I didn't change the subject, Pam would harp on Richard for the rest of the day. "Hmmm. I wonder where my clerks are. I haven't seen them in the last twenty minutes," I said.

"Relax. You've trained them so well you know they're not somewhere goofing off," Pam replied with a dismissive wave.

My job as a senior workshop coordinator was to help organize the classes and make sure everything went smoothly on the clerical end. The three administrative assistants I supervised shared a large cubicle right outside my office. Marybeth Kirby and Ramona Gonzalez were cute brunettes in their mid-twenties. Both were engaged to be married next year. Thirty-two-year-old Sandy Woolrich was a stout redhead who was expecting her first child next year. All three had been with the company for several years. As efficient as they were, I had to monitor their movements from time to time to make sure they didn't take advantage of my laid-back management style. Marybeth and Ramona spent a lot of company time working on their wedding plans. They always met their deadlines, so I let that slide. Sandy browsed baby websites, but only on her breaks and at lunchtime. Marybeth and Ramona had already alerted me that they probably would not stick around too much longer after they got married. Sandy was going to resign when she gave birth and become a stay-at-home mom. Having to break in new employees was one of the few things I didn't like about my job. I wanted to hang on to my current staff as long as possible, so I was pretty lenient with them.

When we entered the break room, all three of my clerks occupied a table near the entrance, chatting like magpies. Every other table was taken. I cleared my throat and glanced at my watch. They stopped talking and abruptly stood up.

"Fel! We were just leaving," Sandy said in a nervous tone as she raked her plump fingers through her hair. "You and Pam can have this table."

I held up my hand. "That's okay. We're going to take our coffee back to my office."

The three women left the table anyway and scurried out of the room like squirrels. "My goodness, Fel. Maybe you trained them too well. Sometimes they act like robots," Pam remarked.

"They're the best support staff I've had since I joined the company," I said proudly.

"No wonder you have such a cushy job."

"I don't know about that. I have a lot of responsibilities," I reminded.

One of my responsibilities was to provide lunch for the people attending our classes. We had a great budget for that, so I had contracts with some of the best caterers in town. I always ordered enough food for myself and my clerks. That pacified them and saved them money. They were so loyal, I didn't have to worry about them leaving me in a lurch. Marybeth and Ramona had promised to hang around after they got married until I hired replacements for them. Or until they got pregnant. That was another thing; women almost young enough to be my daughters were getting married left and right. I'd even been a bridesmaid in two of my former clerks' weddings. I was happy for them, but every now and then I felt like I was being left behind.

By the time we got to my work area, all three of my clerks were pecking away on their computers. Pam closed my door and sat in one of the two large chairs facing my desk.

I ignored the flashing message-waiting light on my landline. I plopped down into my seat and took a sip from my cup. "You didn't have to shut the door, Pam."

"Yes, I did. I don't want anybody to hear what I'm going to say."

"What? If this is about what I told you on the bus this morning or anything else about Richard—"

"Fel, I would love to see you and my baby boy get together, but I know that's not about to happen." Pam paused and gave me a weary look. "Clyde wouldn't know how to keep a woman like you happy."

"What's that supposed to mean?"

She sighed and shook her head. "My son is too immature for a woman like you. No wonder his wife took off and he can't keep a girlfriend for more than a few weeks. You and Richard are perfect for each other."

I gave Pam a thoughtful look and bit my bottom lip. "I'm glad to hear you say that," I admitted. "You just made my day." I couldn't stop myself from smiling.

Instead of smiling back, Pam gave me a pitiful look. "You deserve to be happy. Life is short, Felicia. Don't pass up a good thing. Let Richard know how you feel about him."

I inhaled with my mouth open. "No way. I could never be that forward. I don't chase after men. I never have, and I never will."

"Who said anything about chasing? If you see something you want, go after it. I did."

"You did what?"

"When I realized I wanted to spend the rest of my life with Carlton, I let him know. He's no dreamboat in the looks department, but he's beautiful on the inside and that's more important to me than looks. We belonged to the same church and lived in the same neighborhood all our lives, so I got to know him real well over the years. When we were teenagers, he dated a lot of girls and I dated a lot of boys. By the time we finished high school, I realized he was the best man for me."

"And how did he feel about you?"

"Even though we attended some of the same social events and he took me out a few times, he had never shown any romantic interest in me. We were more like brother and sister. Like you and Richard, and you and Clyde. But when I found out he was planning to join the army, I didn't want to risk losing him. A lot of the boys I knew were being shipped to Vietnam, and a couple didn't come back." At this point, Pam paused and blinked hard. "A month before Carlton left for boot camp, I asked him to marry me."

"What did he say?"

Pam sniffed and kissed her wedding ring. "Isn't it obvious? Why else would I be wearing this ring? He was surprised when I proposed, but he didn't waste any time accepting my proposal. We got married three days before he left. I was proud that he was willing to fight for our country, and God answered my prayers and sent him home in one piece in time for the birth of our first child."

I swallowed hard. "That's a touching story, Pam. I'm glad you shared it with me."

She pursed her lips and gave me a wistful look. "I'm glad you shared your feelings about Richard with me. I hope things work out between you and him."

"I have no idea how he feels. He's been a great *platonic* friend for so long, I don't want to ruin things by telling him I'm in love with him."

"Why not?"

"Seriously? You and I have seen enough movies and read enough romance novels to know that's one of the quickest ways to spook a man and end a good relationship. I'll never tell

Richard I'm in love with him. If all he's ever going to be is a good friend and coworker, I'll have to settle for that."

"I hope you think about it some more and then make the right decision."

"I've already made the right decision. If he has feelings for me, other than as a friend, he would have let me know by now after all the years he's single."

CHAPTER 10

RICHARD

The cafeteria in our building had a great menu and the food was excellent. It was a little pricey, but I still ate lunch in it at least two or three times a week. There were a lot of other places to eat that were within walking distance; and with Cleveland being so close, we had a lot of options.

Several of my male friends worked in the vicinity, so I occasionally went to lunch with them. With all the holiday activity going on, it had been a couple of weeks since I'd spent time with Steven Pardee, my closest male friend. Steven owned a house in Cleveland and worked as a loan manager at Mandell National Bank directly across the street from us. He'd been my best man and his wedding gift to us had been an all-expenses-paid two-week honeymoon in Mexico City. He'd also been one of Margaret's pallbearers. "Hey, brother," he greeted when I dialed his number. "What's up?"

"How was your Thanksgiving, Steven?"

"Well, it was nice but not what I expected. Our oven conked out before the turkey finished cooking and we had a dozen guests coming."

"What did you and Cynthia do when they arrived?"

"Oh, they were all very understanding. We offered to treat everybody to dinner at that buffet on Pike Street. It was the only place we could get a reservation for such a large group. My cousin Jimmy and his wife and son decided to go eat at her folks' house, but everybody else wanted to go to the buffet. Jimmy's brother DeShawn, the wrestler, went through the line so many times, the manager threatened to make me pay for him again."

"I thought it was an all-you-can-eat-for-one-price place?"

"It is! But that's for normal people. Jimmy's monthly grocery bill is more than his mortgage."

"Tell me about it. I'll never forget how much he ate at my Memorial Day cookout last year.

That was the first time we didn't have any leftovers to eat the next day."

We laughed. "So, what are you up to today?" he asked.

"I was hoping you could come over and have lunch with me in our cafeteria. Or we could go someplace else as long as I'm back by one."

"I wish I could go. I'm about to go into our weekly staff meeting in a few minutes and they never end before two. Want to hook up after work for a beer or two?"

"Not today. I drove in and I want to dodge as much of the commute traffic as possible, so I'll be taking off right at five."

"I heard that. Well, maybe we can have lunch later in the week."

"That's cool. I'll talk to you later." I didn't bother to call any of my other friends. I went to a Mexican restaurant on the next block. Five minutes after I sat down with my two beef burritos and Diet Coke, somebody tapped my shoulder.

"Do you mind if I share your table?" It was Regina. She worked as an accountant for a construction company two blocks over, so we often ran into each other on our breaks. She had a tray that contained two tacos and a tall glass of iced tea. As usual, she was dressed to the nines.

"By all means." Even though there were three

other empty chairs at my table, she plopped down in the one next to me. "Did you get your car taken care of?"

"Thank God, I did. But I've decided to trade it in real soon. I don't want to get bamboozled by a sly car salesman and end up with another lemon, so I might bug you to go car shopping with me."

"Uh . . . yeah." I scratched my neck and looked around the room.

"I know you're probably as busy as I am, so I'll wait until January or February. Unless you're available this Saturday."

"No, I won't be. I promised Marva and Carol we'd put up our tree earlier than we did last year. We're going tree shopping first thing Saturday morning. After that we're going to get some of our other shopping out of the way."

"Hey! I was going to do the same thing. Mind if I tag along?"

People accused me of being too nice and passive for my own good, which was the reason I usually got myself in situations I would rather have avoided. But this time, I decided to be a little more assertive. "I'm sorry. The girls made me promise we'd spend some quality time doing fun things alone that day."

"Oh. Well, I can understand that. I probably wouldn't have enough spare time anyway. I'll be busy getting my house in order. Brad Burris—

the man I was with when I ran into you at the steak house last month—he's coming over either Saturday or Sunday to help me hang my outside lights. You know how I always like to have the most lavishly decorated house on the block every Christmas. And I can't do it all by myself."

I nodded. "Uh-huh. I helped you decorate your house last year," I said, groaning at the thought of how I'd spent several hours that day catering to Regina. We laughed. I don't know what made me look around the room but when I did, I spotted Felicia and Pam at a table near the front.

Regina and I finished our orders and got up to leave. I had paid for my lunch when I picked it up, but she still had to pay for hers. We had to walk past the cashier to get to the exit, so we headed in the same direction. Before we reached the counter, she stopped in her tracks. "Oh my God! I just remembered I have only two dollars on me until I go to the bank this afternoon. Richie, can you get me on this one?"

"No problem." Felicia probably wouldn't have even noticed me if Regina had not grabbed ahold of my arm and started giggling about how embarrassed she was about not bringing enough money to cover her lunch. Before we reached the exit, with her still holding my arm and giggling loud enough for people to hear, Felicia turned her head and gazed around the room with a preoccupied expression on her face. When she saw me, her head stopped turning. I nodded. She gave me a weak nod and an even weaker smile.

"Look who's here," Regina whispered. Before I could respond, she did the last thing I wanted her to do: She steered me in Felicia's direction.

CHAPTER 11
FELICIA

I suddenly lost my appetite and my breath caught in my throat as Regina and Richard approached.

I inhaled out of astonishment and whispered, "Oh no! They're coming this way."

"You be nice now," Pam advised.

I was so glad I had on my new black padded Stella McCartney jacket, matching boots, and one of my cutest winter dresses. My makeup couldn't have looked better if a professional had applied it. I didn't feel the least bit nervous this time. When they stopped by the side of our table, I greeted them with the widest smile my lips could form.

"Ladies." Richard looked directly at me and nodded again. "Enjoying your lunch?"

"You'd better believe it. This place serves the best Mexican food in town," Pam replied, purposely bumping my knee with hers.

"Hi again, Felicia," Regina chirped. She cleared her throat and glanced at Pam. "Your name's Pam, right?"

"Every day," Pam replied in a dry tone. "Is it cold enough for you two?"

"Too cold," Richard said with a frown and a shudder.

"Pffftt. This is nothing compared to Alaska where I used to live." Regina paused and snapped her fingers. "We'd call this a warm day." She adjusted the knitted cap on her head and gazed at me, as if sizing me up. "Felicia, it was nice seeing you again so soon. I wish we'd known you two were here sooner. We could have shared a table and chatted for a while."

"Maybe next time," I responded, still displaying my wall-to-wall smile.

"Well, I'd better get back to my office before Sam panics," Richard told us with an exasperated look on his face.

"I have so much work on my desk, we'll be leaving in a few minutes too," Pam stated.

"Me too. I have a conference call to L.A. coming up in about an hour," Regina announced as she pulled Richard away. She held on to his arm like she was afraid he'd leave without her.

They didn't wait for us to say anything else. We watched until they walked out the door.

"Well!" Pam snapped.

"Well what?"

She bit off a chunk of her burrito and didn't answer until she'd chewed and swallowed it. "I think they look mighty cozy."

"If they are 'cozy,' so what?"

Pam reared back in her seat and glared at me. "Is that all you have to say? I thought you were in love with that man."

I hunched my shoulders. "I am." I had no idea how a woman as strong as I was managed to sound so meek. "He's got so many other female friends vying for his attention he's probably not interested in adding another one. Least of all, me."

Pam rolled her neck and snapped her fingers. "You don't know what's on Richard's mind."

I gave her a woeful look and let out a loud breath. "I doubt if it's me. Almost every time I go near his workstation, I see one of those young secretaries on his floor prancing back and forth in front of his office. The day before Thanksgiving, I saw him having lunch in the cafeteria with the one that resembles Beyoncé."

"JoAnn Meecham? Pffftt! Don't worry about

her. I know for a fact she's trying to use Richard to get to his buddy Steven who works in the bank across the street."

"He's married!" I wailed. "I met him and his wife at Richard's wife's funeral."

"So? Some women have no shame. If she's brazen enough to go after a married man, you could at least be brazen enough to go after one who is very much available."

"How many more times do I have to tell you I want to keep Richard as a friend? There is no telling what he might think if he ever finds out how I feel about him. It could make him uncomfortable, not to mention what a fool I'd feel like. I'd have to start riding a later or earlier bus to and from work to avoid him. And anyway, you rarely hear about a relationship between two people who work close together working out."

"Ha! My sister Della and her husband were working for the same factory when they got together. They've been married for twenty-five years and still work at the same place. I know other folks who worked together and got together and are still together. Why don't you invite Richard over for dinner?"

"I've done that already," I said quickly.

"When?"

"Last Christmas Eve, remember?"

Pam gave me an incredulous look and waved

her hand. "There were two dozen other folks at your party, including me, his daughters, and one of those women who works in our payroll department."

"I invited him to my Super Bowl party two years ago and he came—without a date."

"Girl, please. A dozen other folks and I were at that same party. I'm talking about you inviting just him over. In all these years, you've *never* been alone with him."

"What about the day I went with him to the jewelry store on our lunch hour to help pick out something for his daughter? A few weeks after that, I went there with him again to help him find something for his mother-in-law. Each time he told me to pick out something that I'd choose for myself. That way he knew it would be something very nice. He and I were alone those times."

"That doesn't count. You were on company time. You should invite him, nobody else, to have dinner with you at your place."

"Maybe I'll think about that sometime in the future. But I'm not sure it's a good idea to invite him to my house while he's so into Regina."

Pam exhaled and gave me a pensive look. "You may have a point there. Maybe she is 'the one' for him."

"Maybe she is," I agreed.

"Oh well. Maybe it is better if you just remain friends with him."

I gave Pam a puzzled look. "Why did you suddenly change your tune? I thought you wanted to see us together as a couple."

"I did. I mean, I do. But keep in mind that nice friends don't always make nice mates. If things stay the way they are between you two, he'll always be a friend. In some cases, that's better than an intimate relationship . . ."

"I hadn't thought about that," I admitted.

CHAPTER 12

RICHARD

I groaned when I saw all the new voice and e-mail messages waiting for me when I returned to my office. I didn't know where to begin. And they ran the gamut. My cousin Helene had left a voice mail gushing about a "great lady" she wanted to introduce to me at her Christmas Eve party. She'd be one of the last ones I called back.

After I'd responded to five of the eight other voice mail messages, my desk phone rang and Pam's name appeared on the caller ID. I answered her call right away. "Yes, Pam."

"Richard, would you like to help organize our office Christmas party?"

"Sure. That would be fun. You can count on me."

"I knew I could but I wanted to confirm it with you anyway. By the way, how was your lunch today?"

"It was nice, Pam. Thank you for asking."

"That Regina is so stunning."

"Yes, she is. Um, can we talk later? I have a lot of things going on right now."

"Okay. I'll see you on the bus this evening—no, you drove in. I'll see you on the bus tomorrow morning."

"Bye, Pam." I hung up and listened to the next message. In a frantic voice, Sam told me he had left his credit card at the cafeteria where he'd eaten lunch today. He wanted me to retrieve it because he was expecting some important calls and couldn't leave his office for a while (I couldn't wait for his secretary to return!).

There were several messages from coworkers who needed technical assistance with their devices. A pushy secretary in the payroll department had left one inviting me to attend the upcoming Christmas Eve party she was hosting at one of our most popular bars. The other messages were even more mundane, so I saved them for later. Regina had left a message thanking me for "treating" her to lunch today and wanted to know when she could treat me. I shook my head. As much as I liked her, I knew that someday I would just have to be blunt and tell her to back off and quit trying to make something out of nothing. She had several other men on her roster, so I couldn't understand why she gave me so much attention. It seemed like the only person I hadn't heard from was Felicia.

I sat at my desk and stared off into space for a few seconds before I pushed everything on my mind to the side and focused on Felicia. She had seen me with Regina twice since last Friday. There was no telling what she thought about that. Like so many other folks, she probably thought there was something serious going on between Regina and me.

My feelings for Felicia seemed to get stronger each day. Being in her presence made me feel warm all over. But riding with her on the commuter bus, interacting with her at the office, and having lunch or coffee with groups that included her (we'd never even had coffee alone) was no longer enough. It was time to move beyond our friendship. I was going to ask her to have lunch with me tomorrow. At least that would be a start.

My brother, Alex, had left a message that his first son had been born a few hours ago. I called him back immediately. "You rascal, you! You finally did it!" I hollered when he picked up on the second ring. "Congratulations!"

"Thank God it happened before I got too old." Alex was only four years older than me, but he'd been complaining about being "old" since he was in his thirties. "Poor Tina," he went on. "She was in labor for forty-eight hours and I haven't slept a wink myself since it started," he groaned. It was so nice to hear his voice. It had been two weeks since our last conversation. "Richie, I am the happiest man on the planet!" he yelled. "I don't care if I die tomorrow. My life is complete now."

"Whoa now," I cautioned. "If you die tomorrow, what's going to happen to that beautiful family of yours?" I teased.

"You know what I mean. I have fulfilled all of my dreams. What more could a man ask for? And my son—we named him Cyril after my father-in-law—looks exactly like me."

I laughed. "Well, I won't hold that against him." After updating each other on a few things Alex said, "The only thing I want now is for you to be as happy as I am."

"I've never been happier, bro. I have everything a man could want too." I immediately wished I hadn't made that last statement. It could trigger questions and comments I didn't want to hear.

"I am pleased to hear you say that. You're a good man and you deserve to have everything you want." I knew Alex was tuning up his tongue to ask about my love life. I was not interested in discussing the specifics of my love life. Not so long as I was in such a slump and pining away for a woman who had no interest in me except as a seatmate on a bus and a coworker. As much as I enjoyed talking to my brother, I had to cut the call short. I was not in the mood to listen to him go off on a rant about how I needed to find a good woman.

"Brother, you sound tired, so I want you to get some rest. And I have numerous projects I need to attend to today. We'll talk some more real soon. Congratulations again. I hope to come for a visit this summer. My two little queens have been badgering me to bring them down there so you can teach them to dive."

"Well, my home is your home. You and the girls can come anytime and as often as you want. I just picked up some Christmas cards so I'll include pictures of my son in yours. Take care now."

Two seconds after I ended the call, Marva called me on my landline. "Daddy, did you get the message I left on your cellphone?" she asked.

"No, Your Majesty. I've been so busy I haven't had time to check my cellphone. I've told you and your sister that when you can't reach me on my cell at work, call my landline."

"That's what I'm doing. I called to remind you that you have an appointment with Dr. Lowell this afternoon to get your flu shot. You're supposed to be there in an hour and a half."

"Huh? Is that today?"

"I told you I made the appointment for Monday."

"I thought you meant next Monday."

"No, I meant this one. And don't you dare try and sneak off and 'forget' to go like you did last year."

"Okay. I'll see you when I get home this evening."

I hung up and went to the cafeteria to retrieve Sam's wallet. When I got back to my office, I returned some of the other calls and answered a couple of the e-mails. Shortly after that, Sam stumbled into my office to collect his wallet. "Rich, I tell you, being fifty is no walk in the park. It's wreaking havoc with my memory. This is the second time this month I've left my wallet on a counter somewhere," he grumbled as he mopped sweat off his forehead with the back of his hand. "I'm lucky some folks are honest enough to return lost property. Thank you for picking it up."

"No problem. I needed to stretch my legs anyway. Now if you don't mind, I need to duck out a little early. I have a doctor's appointment." I didn't even wait for Sam to respond. I grabbed my coat and we walked out together. When we reached Pam's office, she looked up from her desk with an edgy expression on her face and waved with both hands. Sam liked to chitchat as much as she did, so he entered her office, but I kept moving. I stopped dead in my tracks when Felicia stepped out of the elevator.

"Hi again, Richard," she said in that sweet tone of hers. "Do you know if Pam is in her office?"

"She is. She's talking to Sam," I said quickly as I kept moving. I should have invited her to have lunch with me tomorrow right then and there. But if she'd said no or hemmed and hawed the way some women did when they didn't want to be alone with a particular man, it would have ruined my evening. I'd made up my mind, though. I was going to make my move on her before I lost my nerve. And to keep myself from falling on my face, I'd take baby steps until I felt more comfortable. I just didn't know when I was going to do it.

* * *

After I'd received my flu shot, Dr. Lowell had a cancellation, so he had time to give me my routine checkup, which wasn't due for another month. Afterward, he assured me I was in great shape. "I wish all of my patients were as diligent and health-conscious as you are. You would not believe how many of them are still smoking, drinking like fish, and eating like hogs," he told me in a weary tone as he smoothed back his bushy white hair.

"Well, I wouldn't dream of abusing my body. Too many people depend on me," I stated as I buttoned my shirt.

His tone perked up immediately. "How are the girls?"

I took a deep breath before I answered. "Other than the usual growing pains today's parents have to deal with, I can't complain. I have everything under control," I bragged. "They are very happy with the way things are."

Dr. Lowell scratched his fleshy cheek and peered at me over the top of his glasses. "Are *you* happy with the way things are?"

"Of course. Why do you ask?"

He gave me a skeptical look. "Richard, I've been taking care of you since you were in middle school, so I know you almost as well as I know my own children. You've changed a lot since Margaret passed. That ... um ... spark that used to be in your eyes every time you came in, and when I'd run into you on the street; it's been missing for a long time."

"People do change. Spark or not, I'm still a very happy and lucky man."

"Do you ever plan to remarry?"

The question caught me completely off guard. "Yes, I do," I told him. And I meant every word.

CHAPTER 13
Felicia

I was entering the reviews for last week's classes into our company-wide database when Pam waltzed into my office at three p.m. I was glad to see her holding a Styrofoam tray with two cups of coffee. For somebody who always had "so much work" on her desk she sure had a lot of free time to visit my workstation, as well as other coworkers'. But I always enjoyed Pam's company and her harmless chatter was entertaining. "I thought you'd like a cup of coffee too," she said. She set one of the cups in front of me and then sat down.

"Thank you. I can't talk long, though. I need

to get all this information into the system before I leave today."

Pam took a long pull from her cup before she spoke again. She cleared her throat first and then gave me a wistful look. "I hope Richard is not coming down with something."

"Why would you think that?" I took a sip of my coffee and started typing again.

"Sam told me that he left a little while ago because he had a doctor's appointment. I hope it's nothing serious. It would be a shame for him to get sick this close to Christmas." She paused and cleared her throat again. "By the way, I had a little telephone chat with him before he left. He said he'd love to help organize the office holiday luncheon."

I gulped, stopped typing, and swiveled my chair around so I could look straight in Pam's eyes. "I'm in charge of that this year!" I wailed.

"Choosing a good menu, the right decorations, and a location that'll please most of the attendees, is a lot of work for one person."

"I thought you were going to help me!"

"I was. But I have so much work on my desk that I need to finish before the end of the year, I won't have much time to spare. I hope you don't mind my recruiting Richard."

"Even if I did, what good would it do now?" I

let out a heavy sigh. "I shouldn't have told you about my feelings for him. Something tells me you are trying to play matchmaker."

"Fel, whatever goes on between you and Richard is none of my business."

I shook my head. "Thanks. Now, if you don't mind, I need to get back to work."

"I do too. I have so much work on my desk."

Richard and Pam were in their usual spots when I got on the bus this morning. Today's weather was pretty cold, and everybody was swaddled in so many layers of clothing, they looked like cocoons. "Happy Tuesday, girl," Pam greeted, adjusting the brown muffler wrapped around her neck.

"Hi, Pam." I eased down with caution next to Richard, but my knee touched his anyway. "Good morning, Richard. Pam told me you wanted to help plan the office Christmas party this year."

He nodded. "In any way I can. I already have a few ideas about how we can make it more festive this year."

"I hope so. That little thing we did at the Italian bistro last year was so boring," Pam chimed in.

"Are you ladies available for lunch today? We can discuss it in more detail then."

Pam didn't waste any time responding. "No

day this week is good for me. My daughter-in-law is coming to have lunch with me today. I'll probably work through lunch the rest of the week because I have so much work on my desk. But you two can go ahead and get started." She looked at me with a mischievous expression on her face.

"We don't have to do it during lunch, Richard. I don't want you to give up your personal time. I can come to your office or you can come to mine and we can figure things out. You can even send me your ideas by e-mail," I suggested.

"I don't know about your section. But mine is so busy, I have very little time to spare during company hours. I'd prefer getting together at lunchtime," Richard said. "I'll check my schedule and get back to you as soon as possible."

"That'll be fine, Richard."

At the next stop, a regular commuter sat down in the seat in front of Richard and me and started talking to him like he hadn't seen him in years. Another chatty rider sat down next to Pam and started yakking away, so that took her out of the equation. Their subjects didn't interest me, so I opened my newspaper and read until we reached our destination.

We had a five-day class starting today. By the time I got to my work area, my clerks had already stacked the brochures and handouts in the hallway racks outside the largest of our three training rooms. I stopped in the doorway of my clerks' cubicle. "Good morning, ladies. Are we all set for today's class?"

"Morning, Fel. Everything is good to go. We just set up the equipment for the PowerPoint presentation," Ramona told me. "Dennis Kline called in sick, so Mark Cramer will be facilitating the class today."

"And I just confirmed everything with the caterer. That pasta dish I ordered for our last class was so popular with our trainers and attendees, I ordered it again for today," Marybeth tossed in.

"Good work!" I exclaimed, giving a thumbs-up. I got situated at my desk and started checking messages. Richard had left a voice mail a few minutes ago. "Felicia, I'm really looking forward to having lunch with you." I wondered why he was so eager to have lunch with me just to discuss plans for our Christmas party.

I called him back right away and he answered on the first ring. "Hello, Richard. Is tomorrow a good day for lunch?" I quickly added, "To discuss our Christmas party."

"That's fine. I can't wait to share my ideas with you."

"Oh? Like what?" As much as I cared about Richard, I was hoping he would give me enough information over the phone so I wouldn't need to have lunch alone with him. The more I thought about it, the more nervous I felt.

"Last year's party was pretty dull. Except for the Christmas tree and a few decorations, it seemed like any other day. I thought a gift exchange would be nice this year. And how about a deejay to spin some holiday tunes?"

"You don't think that's a little too much for a lunchtime event?"

"Yes, I do. That's why I think we should plan something for after work hours."

"I like those ideas. What about the menu?"

"We'll decide on the food later. But we can't go wrong with a buffet."

"Pam suggested that too. She wants it to be potluck so everybody can bring a dish."

"I think that's a wonderful suggestion, but we should also have a few items catered. The more choices people have, the happier they'll be. Besides, some people don't like to cook unless they have to, so let's give them some options."

"I'm sure one of the caterers we already use would love to accommodate us. I've already checked with Sam and he thinks we should have our event no later than the week before Christmas, Tuesday the eighteenth."

"That sounds like a reasonable date. We can finalize everything during lunch tomorrow?"

"Sure, Richard. How about getting together in the cafeteria?"

"Uh-uh. Too noisy and crowded. How about that little deli on the next block?"

With each word that came out of his mouth, I asked myself, what am I getting myself into? I was infatuated with this man and was nervous about being alone with him in public. I was afraid I'd let my guard down and reveal my true feelings to him. The thought of that happening chilled me to the bone.

"Okay. Just let me know what time." My heart was beating so hard, it felt like it was going to explode. Before he could say another word, I hung up and made a mad dash to the ladies' room so I could compose myself.

CHAPTER 14
FELICIA

When I left the ladies' room, I decided to visit Pam's office. "Why is that weary look on your face?" she asked when I shuffled in and sat down.

"I'm having lunch with Richard tomorrow. He wants to go to that little deli you and I went to last week. I don't know how I'm going to make it through that lunch without making myself look like a fool."

"Felicia, I know you're younger than me, but you are not that young. You sound like a schoolgirl! What's the big deal? Most women would love to eat lunch with a man they're in love with."

"Yes, but this one-sided situation is wearing me out. I wish he would do or say something to turn me off so I could get him out of my system."

Pam laughed. "I wish I could be a fly on the wall at that deli tomorrow so I could watch you squirm."

"That's not funny," I scolded. "I have never felt this way about a man. It's disturbing."

Pam gave me a concerned look. "You're really serious, aren't you?"

I nodded. "Sometimes I wish I didn't have to see him every day."

"Well, you might not have to see him every day too much longer."

That comment threw me for a loop. I squinted my eyes at Pam and asked, "What do you mean?"

"Working in personnel, I always get a heads-up on things going on at this company." Pam nodded toward the door and I got up and closed it.

"What's going on?" I whispered. I returned to my seat and scooted it closer to her desk.

"I saw a memo a little while ago. Sam's been raving so much about how efficient and dependable Richard is, the home office honchos want him to come over there and manage their tech support staff. The guy who has been doing the job for twenty-two years is going to retire in January."

"Richard would have to move to Indianapolis," I muttered.

"Exactly."

I stared blankly ahead for a few moments. When I returned my attention to Pam, I was surprised to see a puppy-dog expression on her face. I had a feeling I had the same look on my face. "I'll miss him," I mumbled.

"Me too. But let's not jump to conclusions. I don't even know if they've approached him about it yet."

I stood up. "Thanks for letting me know."

"If he knew how you felt about him, he'd probably think twice about relocating."

I gave Pam a thoughtful look. "Well, his not being around would sure bring me back to my senses." I started inching toward the door.

"Girl, there is so much work on my desk. I probably won't see you again until we get on the bus this evening."

I had to finish a project for Sam before the end of the day, so I missed the bus I usually took home and caught a later one. When I got off at my stop and walked the block to my apartment building, I was pleased to see so much mail in my box. As usual, it was mostly advertisements and bills. Among the five early Christmas cards was one from my brother. I was always happy to hear from him. Another piece of mail that made me smile was a beautiful postcard from my parents in Nairobi, Kenya. It contained a picture of them on the back standing next to a zebra in a straw hat and sunglasses. I was overcome with emotion as I rode the elevator up to my apartment. I blinked to hold back my tears when Lorena opened her door and leaned out. "Hey, Fel. Want to come over and keep me company?"

"I'll let you know later. Right now I'd like to see if I can catch up with my brother. I received a Christmas card from him today and I'd like to let him know. And I promised my grandmother I'd take her out to dinner this evening. If it's not too late when I get home, I'll come over."

I caught Victor at a bad time. "Hey, sis. I can't chat right now. I'm on my way out the door to meet with a very important client. Anyway, I received a cute postcard from the folks posing with a zebra in Kenya."

"They sent me the same one." We laughed. "Send me a text or call and let me know when you want to have a nice long video chat."

"Will do. How's Grandma Lucy?"

"Same old, same old. Oh! Thank you for the Christmas card. I received it today. I'll be sending mine in the next couple of weeks. You take care and tell the family I said hello."

Clyde had left a voice mail message to remind me that I'd promised to go out with him this coming weekend. I immediately dialed his number and he answered halfway through the first ring. "I was just about to call you again, Fel," he chirped. "Where do you want to eat Friday night before we go to the movies?"

"Anywhere except Popeye's like the last two times we went out."

"I'm sorry to hear that because I have a coupon for eight pieces of chicken. Well, we can go to Red Lobster if you don't mind footing the bill. I just realized this evening that I'd received my last unemployment check last week. I had to spend all but eight dollars of it to get the brakes on my truck fixed. You would have to pay for the movies, too."

"I'm sorry, Clyde. My finances are pretty tight right now. Why don't we hold off going out for a little while?"

"Okay. I can still come over Friday night and keep you company. You make a mean bowl of popcorn. If you cook enough, we won't have to eat nothing else that night. That'd be a nice way to start off the weekend."

I laughed. "I don't think I'll be in the mood for a popcorn dinner. I have a better idea. We have a class going on through Friday and we always order extra food for the attendees' lunch. If you want to come to my office around one p.m., we can grab a plate and go sit in my office.

That would be a nice way to start off the weekend too."

"That sounds like too much trouble. But I
ain't got no ten or twelve dollars to park in one
of them lots, and I don't do buses. Um, remember that woman I told you I met at the mall?"
Clyde didn't give me time to answer. "She invited me to her house this coming Friday night.
I told her I'd get back to her, but I didn't tell her
I'd already made plans with you. Anyway, she
wants to cook dinner for me. Since me and you
won't be getting together, I guess I'll take her up
on it."

"Clyde, do whatever you want to do. I have
plenty to do to keep myself busy."

It saddened me a little to know that my position with Clyde was not so secure anymore. He
was peculiar but he was fun and a great diversion to keep my mind off the many nights I
spent alone. In the past, when he didn't have
money to take me out, I didn't have a problem
paying or with him coming over and sharing a
bowl of popcorn while we watched TV. A few
other men I occasionally dated hadn't contacted
me in weeks. And when I attempted to contact
them, they never returned my calls. My newest
admirers included a mechanic almost young
enough to be my son and a retired engineer old

enough to be my father. It was hard to believe that this was what my life had come to.

Whenever I invited Grandma Lucy out to eat, each time I suggested an upscale restaurant. However, she almost always chose Denny's, so that's where I took her this evening. Right after a server took our order for burgers and fries, Grandma Lucy started shifting in her seat and patting the sides of her head. She had a lot of wrinkles and skin tags on her face and she was slightly overweight. But she was still attractive. Even in the black cape she had on over a flowered housedress this evening.

"Please sit still and quit fussing with your hair," I advised. Grandma Lucy stopped wiggling but she kept patting her hair.

"I wish I had left this wig-hat at home. It's itching," she complained. Why my grandmother wore a "wig-hat" in the first place was a mystery to me. Her long, thick gray hair was much more attractive. Then she started grinding her teeth. "I wish I had left these darn things at home." Before I could stop her, she removed her upper and lower dentures and set them on the napkin next to her plate.

"People are staring," I said in a low voice as I

looked around. I could feel my face burning with embarrassment.

"So what? My teeth ain't bothering nobody." Grandma Lucy sniffled and narrowed her eyes as she gazed at me. "Now let's talk about something else." She paused, and then a wide smile crossed her face. "I declare, you are so pretty. You look like I did when I was your age. So tell me, did anybody ask you out this week?"

"Not yet." I knew that if I told her about Clyde's request to come over and eat popcorn with me Friday night, it would lead to more comments I didn't want to hear.

"Well, I got a feeling you might have a message from a man waiting on you when you get home."

I did have a message from a man when I got home. Daddy had called to remind me to go pay his property taxes.

CHAPTER 15
RICHARD

"Daddy, I hope you have a good day," Carol told me as we prepared to leave for the day this morning. She was sitting on the couch, pulling on her Ugg boots.

"I'm sure I will. I'm having lunch with a very special lady today." I snatched my overcoat off the rack by the front door and had to force myself not to show how giddy I was.

"Regina?" Marva asked as she entered the living room already bundled up and ready to go.

"I said a very *special* lady." All three of us laughed. "You girls remember Felicia, one of the ladies I work with? We went to her Christmas Eve party last year."

"That party was fun!" Marva gushed. "Felicia hugged us, but she didn't give us any presents. She's real cool, though. We see her a lot all over the place. When we visited Grandma and Grandpa Labor Day weekend, we bumped into Felicia at Olive Garden. We had to wait for a table and when she came in after us by herself, we all stood together by the wall. Grandma and Grandpa must really like her because they got all over her right away—and you know how picky they can be."

"I didn't know they knew her well enough to 'get all over her,'" I said.

Carol gave me an exasperated look as she wrapped her muffler around her neck. "Daddy, you and your memory. They met Felicia at Mama's funeral. She helped serve food when we came home from the church. And did you know that she came to the house a couple of days later to help Grandma and Aunt Minnie pack up Mom's stuff that we didn't want to keep? She even took it to Goodwill because they were too sad to do it."

"I don't remember," I muttered. Margaret's passing had been so traumatic for me, I no longer remembered some of the things that occurred during that period. I did recall Felicia being among the mourners at the church and later at my house, but everything else was a blur.

"Grandpa told Felicia that she and the friend

she was waiting on could sit with us if they wanted to. But she said she'd rather not because she had some personal things she needed to discuss with her friend," Carol went on. "Grandpa got excited when Felicia told him that her brother was a big important private investigator in Atlanta. And he and Grandma were real impressed when she told us how she'd talked her parents into taking the six-month trip around the world they'd planned, instead of canceling it to stay home and take care of Felicia's mom's mother. When the Olive Garden hostess came to escort us to our table, Grandma and Grandpa hugged Felicia and told her she's welcome to come visit them anytime she wants. As we were walking away, I saw a man come in the door and kiss her on the cheek. I guess he was her boyfriend."

"He looked like Steve Harvey did when he still had hair," Marva added.

"That had to be Clyde, the son of one of our coworkers. He and Felicia have been seeing each other for a long time." The next sentence slid out of my mouth before I realized what I was saying. "They're just friends, though," I said stiffly.

"She's so nice," Carol said.

"And pretty," Marva tossed in.

"She sure is. She often asks about you both.

Carol, you should have seen how big her eyes got when I told her you're going to be a lawyer." I paused and turned to Marva and said, "And that you're going to be a judge."

"What did she say?" Marva wanted to know.

"She said I was lucky to have such ambitious kids," I answered, puffing out my chest. "And that she hopes to have kids like you two someday."

"Then she is a 'very special lady,'" Carol said, giving me a mysterious wink. I pretended like I didn't see it.

Felicia was much more than a "very special lady." I promised myself I wouldn't act giddy, or say anything stupid or offensive at lunch today. I didn't want to jeopardize our friendship. Just knowing that my picky in-laws had said so many nice things about her made my head swell. "Okay, queens. Let's shake a leg." I snapped my fingers and nodded toward the door. "I don't want to miss my bus."

To my surprise, Felicia never boarded the bus this morning. When I walked into my office, and before I removed my coat, I called her number and got her voice mail. I left a message and without giving it much thought, I gave her lead clerk a call. I was pleased to hear that Felicia had some business to take care of and that she would be in today.

Pam popped into my office at exactly eleven

a.m. "Richard, I need to talk to you." There was a deadpan expression on her face and her voice sounded very serious. There was no telling what she had up her sleeve. She closed the door before I could respond. I had moved the chair that usually sat in front of my desk to the side of the room. I'd placed a huge stack of files on it, hoping it would discourage visitors from sitting down and staying too long. Pam casually set the files on top of my file cabinet, dragged the chair to the front of my desk, and dropped down. "I hope you don't mind."

"Will this take long? I'm very busy," I said firmly.

"I don't need much time."

"What's going on? Does this have anything to do with technical support or a reprographics issue?" I cleared my throat and narrowed my eyes. "Or is this personnel-related?" Disturbing thoughts suddenly entered my mind. Had I unknowingly done something against company policy? Was I about to lose my job? I immediately dismissed those thoughts. Pam was a secretary. If I had done something inappropriate or was about to get laid off or fired, she wouldn't be the one to tell me.

"This has nothing to do with a personnel issue," she confirmed. "My computer is working fine and all of my copy issues are up-to-date. But there's a lot of work on my desk, so I'll get right to the point so we can both get back to work." She cleared her throat and gazed at me for a few seconds before continuing. "I heard the company is considering you for a position in Indianapolis. A promotion."

"It's tempting. But relocating to another state would be a big step; not just for me, but for my girls. We'd have to make a lot of adjustments."

"Do you know anybody in Indianapolis?"

"Not a soul. Pam, I'm curious and confused. Where is this conversation going?"

"I didn't want to be too blunt. But the more I think about this, the more I want to—" She stopped talking and glanced toward the door. When she turned back around, she looked so hopeless I didn't know what to think.

"Can you wrap this up in the next couple of minutes?" I asked as I checked my watch.

"Felicia is in love with you," she blurted out. If Pam had told me she was going to wrestle a grizzly bear, I couldn't have been more stunned.

I narrowed my eyes and leaned forward. "What did you say?"

"Felicia is in love with you," she repeated. She folded her arms and gave me a guarded look.

I had to force myself not to laugh. "She dates your son and other men. She has no romantic interest in me."

"Oh yes she does! My son, though I love him to death, is just a filler."

"Excuse me?"

"Clyde and the other men she's been dating for the past few years are just filling in because she can't be with the man she really loves. And that's *you*."

"Now, Pam. I know you're a caring person. But this is over the top—even for you. What makes you think Felicia is in love with me?"

"She told me."

I sat up straighter and stared at Pam in slack-jawed amazement. "Excuse me?" I said again.

"I was just as surprised as you. The bottom line is, she's been in love with you for a long time. She was having such a hard time keeping it to herself, she finally broke down and told me."

"And she told you to tell me?"

"Nope. She didn't tell me *not* to tell you, though."

I scratched the side of my head. "I don't know what to say. I never expected to hear something like this."

"I didn't either." Pam stood up and gave me a smug look. "Well, now you know."

"Thanks for sharing with me. But I'd rather hear it from Felicia."

"Don't hold your breath. I don't think she'll ever tell you herself."

"Well, if she told you, why wouldn't she tell me?"

Pam shrugged and started backing toward the door. "Beats me. Anyway, I said what I came to say. Now I need to get back to my office because there is so much work on my desk."

I had a hard time focusing on my work after Pam left. Ten minutes later, Carol called. "Hi, Daddy."

"Hello, queen."

"I'm on my way to my math class so I have to talk fast. Ki Ki Randolph is having a slumber party next Friday. Can we go?"

"We'll talk about that when I get home."

"Daddy, why do we need to talk about it? She lives right next door."

"I need to talk to her mother first. I'm glad you called. I forgot to take the laundry out of the dryer last night. When you get home, take care of it."

"When are you going to talk to Ki Ki's mother? She wants to know how many girls she'll need to buy snacks for."

"I'll call her or go over and see her when I get home."

"She'll like that," Carol snickered.

"What's that supposed to mean?"

"Daddy, you know that lady has been crushing on you ever since they moved next door. She's a widow so you and she have something in common. And don't you think she's pretty?"

"She's a very pretty woman—"

Carol cut me off. "Ooo! Ooo! I can't wait to tell her you said that—"

And then I cut her off. "You behave yourself. I have something in common with a lot of pretty women. End of discussion." I sniffed and added, "You be sure and take those lamb chops out of the freezer like I told you this morning so they can defrost in time for dinner. And don't forget that laundry."

Carol taunted me with a sharp laugh. "Okay, Daddy. I love you."

"Love you back, Your Majesty."

There was only one pretty woman on my mind these days.

CHAPTER 16
FELICIA

I ate a light breakfast Wednesday morning before I drove to the tax collector's office to pay my folks' property taxes. After that, I brought my car back home and took a later bus to the office. I arrived a few minutes before eleven a.m.

I stopped in the doorway of my clerks' cubicle and cleared my throat to get their attention. From the corner of my eye, I saw Sandy quickly minimize whatever was on her computer screen. Marybeth was on her telephone, giggling like a schoolgirl. She suddenly hung up without saying a word and gave me a sheepish look. Ramona fiddled with a manila folder to hide the *Brides* magazine she'd been leafing through. I shook my head and wagged my finger at them. We all laughed. As long as my clerks' antics didn't impact their work performance and they were fairly discreet, I would continue to let them get away with some of the same tricks I'd pulled when I worked as a clerk back in the day.

"Good morning, ladies," I greeted. "Is everything under control?"

"It's all good," Marybeth said with a sniff and a red face. "All the attendees showed up on time and the trainer complimented us on how well we'd set up the classroom."

"Good! Anything else?" I asked.

"That hot Richard Grimes in tech support called me when he couldn't reach you. He was checking to see if you were coming in today," Sandy told me.

"Okay. I'll give his hot self a call," I replied. All three clerks snickered.

Before I could get back to Richard, he called again. I answered on the second ring. "Hi, Richard. Are we still on for lunch today?"

"Absolutely. Noon?"

"Noon is fine. But like I told you before, I don't mind going to the cafeteria."

"If we do go there, I'm sure at least one of our coworkers will invite themselves to sit down at our table."

"That wouldn't bother me."

"Normally, it wouldn't bother me either. But having somebody present who is not involved with the holiday plans would be disruptive. We can get together some other time, some other place."

"No, I'd like to get as much done on this as possible today. How about grabbing something from the cafeteria and meeting in my office, or yours."

"I have a better idea and it'll be my treat. Have you been to that new French bistro that just opened a few blocks from here?"

"I love that place. Pam and I went the day they opened last month. I know it's close by. But because the weather is so bad today, walking a couple of blocks would seem like a couple of miles."

"We'll take a taxi. I'll meet you in the lobby at noon."

I agreed, but with hesitation. "Oh. Okay."

Pam must have been lying in wait because before I could even return the telephone back into its cradle, she entered my office. "What's up?" she asked with raised eyebrows.

"I just got off the phone with Richard. He's treating me to lunch today at Andre's Bistro."

"Humph! He's going to spend a pretty penny in that place. I wish I could go too."

"Well, if you really want to, I'm sure he wouldn't mind. You're supposed to help me finalize the plans for our Christmas lunch anyway. I can call him back and let him know you want to come."

"Girl, go on without me. There is so much work on my desk, I couldn't leave until around twelve thirty." Pam paused and stared at me with a smirk on her face. "Besides, I have a feeling you'd really rather be alone with him and vice versa."

"You stop that!" I scolded. I shook my finger in her face. "I wish you would stop harping on this subject."

She laughed and then abruptly stopped. The serious look that suddenly appeared on her face made me nervous. "I still think you should take my advice and invite him to your place for dinner."

"I don't think so." I glanced over Pam's shoulder, held up my hand, and said in a low voice, "My clerks have big ears and I don't want them to hear what I have to say."

Pam leaped out of her seat and closed my office door so hard and fast, every picture on my wall rattled. "What is it?" she whispered. I remained silent. "You know I have high blood pressure, so don't keep me in suspense." She dropped back into her seat with a thud and a wild-eyed look on her face.

"I've been thinking that it's time for me to make a major change in my life."

Pam looked at me sideways with her eyes narrowed. "What major change?"

"Changing jobs."

She did a double take. "What? Why would you want to leave such a dream job? Do you know how many folks would love to be in your shoes? You're the first black woman to be in this position since I've been with the company, which is going on thirty-five years. You're an inspiration to the young black employees just getting started here. And you know everybody loves you to death! You've been voted employee of the month so many times I've lost count."

"I'm grateful for all that. But I've gone as far as I can go here."

Pam let out a loud breath and gave me a suspicious look. "Does this have anything to do with Richard?"

I had never lied to Pam and I was not going to start now. I nodded.

"But he might be transferring to Indianapolis!"

"What if he doesn't? It's getting harder and harder for me to be around him and not let him know how I feel. I don't know how much longer I can go on like this." I blinked at Pam. "I never knew I could love a man as much as I love Richard. The only way I'm going to get over him is to take myself out of the picture. I spent some time on Google last night. There are a lot of job opportunities for a woman with my background and experience."

"Going to work for another company won't solve your problem. Even if you don't take the same commuter bus to a new job, Mandell is such a small city, you'd still run into Richard from time to time."

"The companies I checked out are all in Atlanta."

Pam gulped and covered her mouth with her hand for a few moments. "Do you mean to tell me that you'd give up this job and move to another state just to avoid Richard?"

"It's not just because of him. My parents told me that they might move to Atlanta when they return. Grandma Lucy is going to go with them, so there wouldn't be much to keep me here."

"You have a lot of cousins in this area."

"Yes, but they're so busy raising their children and interacting with people they have more things in common with than me, I don't spend much time with them."

"Humph. I never expected to hear you talk about leaving Ohio."

"You're going to retire next year, so work won't be the same without you if I stay. And Clyde

told me that you and Carlton have discussed sell-
ing your house and moving in with your daughter and her family *in Houston*."

"Yes, my husband has been hinting about
moving to Houston. But even if we decide to do
that, it wouldn't happen for a while after Carlton and I retire. And he's got another year and a
half to go. Before we could even put the house
on the market, we'd have to get a lot of work
done on it. That wouldn't happen overnight, so
we could live here for another three or four
years."

"Pam, I understand what you're saying. The
bottom line is, almost everybody I know has or is
making plans for their future. I'm just standing
still."

Pam stood up and started moving toward the
door. "I'm glad you shared what's on your mind
with me. But we need to discuss this again when
I have more time. There is so much work on my
desk, I need to get back to my office." She
opened the door and winked. "Enjoy your lunch
with Richard. When we talk later, I want a full report."

CHAPTER 17
RICHARD

At eleven a.m., my best friend strolled into my office. Steven was as thin as a rail and as blind as a bat without the thick glasses that covered his deep-set black eyes. He wore a black knitted cap on his shaved head, a wool coat over a three-piece black suit, and black leather gloves. "Hey! How's my favorite bag of bones! I wasn't expecting you," I hollered, rising from my seat. He moved closer and I leaned forward so we could bump fists. "How's life treating you?"

"Each day is better than the last!" he exclaimed. Steven was the kind of person who always looked on the bright side of things. In all the years I'd known him, I'd never heard him complain. His positive attitude was so contagious, having a friend like him was a blessing. "You've been on my mind a lot lately, so I thought I'd pay you a visit." He paused and gave me a thoughtful look. "One of my meetings got canceled, so I thought I'd pop over here and see if you wanted to join me for lunch. I'm sorry I couldn't hook up with you the other day. You sounded like you really needed to talk."

I waved my hand. "Man, it was nothing. I'd love to accompany you today, but I have something else on my schedule. I wish you had called so you wouldn't have made a trip over here for nothing. Sit down."

"No, that's okay. I'll just pick up something and go back to my office. Maybe I'll come over to your pad in the next few days. I'd love to see the girls."

"Either that or we'll drop in on you and Cynthia and your five rug rats." I heaved out a heavy sigh and shook my head. "Man, I love this time of year, but there is so much going on, I don't know how I'm able to keep up."

"You need a break, my man. Hey, if you're not doing anything this Saturday night, one of Cynthia's sorority sisters—"

I held up my hand to cut him off. "Ouch!" I

yelled with a grimace. "That hurts. I already have too much on my plate in that area."

Steven rolled his eyes and smothered a laugh. "I'm just trying to help, dude." We laughed and bumped fists again. "Well, I guess I'll be on my way so you can get ready for your meeting."

"Um, I don't have a meeting. I'm having lunch with a coworker. You remember Felicia Hawkins."

Steven shook his head. "I'm not sure." Then his eyes got big. "Whoa! Didn't Cynthia and I meet her at Margaret's funeral? She's one of the ladies you've mentioned who rides to and from work with you on the same bus, right?"

I nodded.

Steven whistled and stared at me in awe. "My man! I know some fine-looking women, but Felicia is a cross between Naomi Campbell and Angela Bassett. It doesn't get any better than that. And you get to work with her too. Oomph, oomph, oomph. I hope she's interested in more than your electronic skills. You better be good to her!"

I held up my hands. "Calm down. I'm taking her to lunch, not marrying her."

"Well, I know you'll enjoy having lunch with her. Give me a call when you get a chance," he said as he strolled back out the door.

I looked out the window for a few moments. As close as Steven and I were, I didn't want to tell him how I felt about Felicia. But I didn't know how much longer I could contain myself. Having lunch alone with her today was a major step in the right direction.

At exactly eleven forty-five, Sam steamrolled into my office like somebody was chasing him. "*Mamma mia!* Thank God you're still here," he boomed. "I need your help. All the other technicians have already left for lunch."

"What's the problem?" I asked calmly.

"My computer just died. I may have lost some very important information—the numbers for next year's budget. We have to finalize everything before December thirty-first."

"Can this wait until after lunch? Felicia and I were going to discuss the plans for our Christmas party."

Sam shook his head so hard his long dirty blond and gray hair flopped up and down against the back of his neck. "I'm afraid if I put it off, we may not be able to retrieve the information in time. I never got around to saving it onto a flash drive or my hard drive."

"What about your original notes?"

"I misplaced them or accidentally threw them out!" Sam wailed. From the frantic look on his face, I thought he was going to burst into tears. And I was not in the mood to watch a grown man cry.

"I see. Give me a sec. Let me see if I can postpone my lunch date." I called Felicia's office and got her voice mail. I left a message to let her know something had come up and we'd have to reschedule. And then I followed Sam to his cluttered office.

His computer was dead all right. But only because the power cord had come loose from the wall. When I pointed that out to him, he gave me an embarrassed look and shook his head. "I guess I should have checked that first, huh?"

"You should have," I said, trying to keep my voice gentle. Sam was a highly intelligent guy. He'd graduated with honors from Harvard, but sometimes he was so inept, I felt sorry for him. And he was such a nice guy, no matter how much he irritated me, I always managed to keep my cool. Before I could be on my way, he started telling me about his plans for the weekend. After that, he spent a few minutes bragging about his wife and children. That compelled me to throw in a few praises about my girls. Besides, so much time had passed, I didn't expect Felicia to still be in the lobby. I figured she had gone to lunch on her own and that's what I decided to do. Before I left the building, I swung by her office in case she had returned. She was nowhere in sight, so I headed for the lobby.

Once I reached the ground floor, I buttoned my coat all the way up to my neck and strode out the exit along with a mob of other people. As soon as I got outside, I spotted Regina walking in my direction. Stumbling along on the icy sidewalk with her was a cute young blonde in a red wool coat and a matching wool hat.

"Richard! You're a sight for sore eyes on such a dreary day! Where are you off to?" Regina squealed. I had suspected a long time ago that some of our random encounters were not so random. She knew most of the places I frequently patronized. Somehow she managed to show up at a few at the same time as if she'd been monitoring my movements with a tracking device. Even though I turned down invitations from her left and right, that didn't discourage her. Regina still managed to manipulate me into joining her for one thing or another. She'd even turned up at one of my girls' soccer games and wiggled her way into having dinner at Red Lobster with us afterward.

"Oh, I'm just going to grab a little something to nibble on," I replied, looking around.

"We're on our way to Wing Lu's for dim sum. Rich, this is Susan Snell, my new intern."

"Nice to meet you, Susan," I said, shaking her gloved hand.

"I'm like so glad I finally got to meet you," Susan replied in a Minnie Mouse voice. "Why don't you come with us?"

"Thanks a lot, but I don't want to intrude," I protested with my hand up in the air. "I'm just going to grab something and go eat in my office." I didn't realize until it was too late that my excuse was too weak to ward off Regina.

"Nonsense." She put her arm around my shoulder and ushered me down the street. "That's what you said the last time I invited you to join me for dim sum."

Wing Lu's was on the next block, so it was a short walk. Once we got seated and started plucking things off the dim sum tray, the time seemed to crawl by as slowly as a dying snail.

CHAPTER 18

RICHARD

For each dim sum item I chose, Regina and Susan chose two or three apiece. I had never seen women as slim and dainty as these two eat so much and so fast. I ordered tea, they ordered wine and mineral water.

We were having a lively conversation, discussing our plans for Christmas and a few other unrelated subjects. However, only fifteen minutes later, my level of boredom was almost as high as the ceiling. After three cups of green tea, I had to make a beeline for the men's room. "Excuse me, ladies. I'll be back in a few minutes," I said, rising quickly. I glanced at my watch as I trotted across the floor.

I returned to the dining area just in time to hear Susan say to Regina, "I'd like, walk through fire in my bare feet to have a man like Richard. He's awesome. I'm glad you decided to claim him again." Those words stopped me in my tracks. I ducked behind the wall facing our table and listened. "I'm like, surprised he still speaks to you. Especially after you dumped him while he was risking his life in the military."

"Pfffft. He's too sweet and nice to hold a grudge. In all the years I've known him, I've never seen him get angry or even raise his voice."

"Do you think he still loves you?"

"I'm sure he does."

"Then why aren't you two in a more serious relationship than just these casual encounters you keep telling me about?"

"Richard is just being cautious this time. He'll come around eventually."

They abruptly stopped talking when I approached the table. "Well, ladies, this was nice, but I need to get back to my office."

Regina looked at her watch and gasped. "We have to get going too. Before I go, Richard, I wanted to let you know that every Tuesday they serve those spicy pot stickers here that you like so much."

"Then I'll have to come back here on a Tuesday," I said casually. I lifted the check off the table. Wing Lu's was not cheap, so the $155 total didn't surprise me.

"How much do I owe?" Susan asked.

I held up my hand. "Don't worry about it. This is on me."

"Thanks, Richard," Regina said as she picked her teeth with a toothpick. "You are too sweet." From the corner of my eye, I saw Susan stare at Regina in awe.

When we started walking toward the exit, Regina latched on to my arm. Susan was in front of us, picking her teeth too. I tapped her on the shoulder. "Do you mind if I speak privately to Regina for a few minutes?"

"Sure! Regina, I'll see you back at the office," Susan chirped. "This was a great lunch," she added, looking at me. From the corner of my eye, I saw Susan wink at Regina. I glanced away because I didn't want to see how Regina responded to that.

As soon as Susan skittered out the door, I removed Regina's hand from my arm. I took her hand in mine, steered her off to the side, and placed my hands on her shoulders. I looked her straight in the eyes. "Regina, we've been friends for over twenty years."

There was a glazed look on her face. "Twenty good years," she said, practically swooning.

"You were my first love," I admitted. She started blinking so hard, I was surprised she didn't blink her eyelashes off. Then she sniffled a few times and gently rubbed her nose. For a second, I thought she was going to shed a few tears. "I still care about you, but not the way you think."

She wheezed and stared at me in slack-jawed amazement. And then her face looked as if it had suddenly turned to stone. "You . . . you heard Susan and me talking?"

"I heard enough. I hope I don't sound too blunt, but I can't let you go on thinking what you think."

She gave me an incredulous look and re-moved my hands from her shoulders. "Are you telling me you no longer want to be friends with me?"

"We can always be friends, but that's all."

Her lips quivered and she rubbed her nose again. "Can I ask you something and will you be honest with me?"

"I've always been honest with you."

"Is there another woman?"

"Yes, there is. I'm very serious about her."

Regina gasped and stumbled a few feet away. "W-when did this happen?"

"I've been serious about her for years."

"I see," she said in a very small voice. She

looked so glum, I felt sorry for her. "If I had known, I wouldn't have wasted my time, or yours—"

I held my hand up and cut her off as fast as I could. "You never wasted my time and I'm sorry you feel as if you've wasted yours. I couldn't go on letting you think that there was a chance for us to be something more than friends."

She gazed at the floor for a few seconds. When she returned her attention to me, there was a broad smile on her face. "Whoever she is, she is a lucky woman."

"And I'm a lucky man."

She walked ever so slowly up to me and gave me a quick peck on the cheek and patted my shoulder. I exhaled and pulled her into my arms. We embraced until an incoming patron entered about ten seconds later and mumbled, "Get a room." I released her and we laughed. And then she looked at peace, which made me feel better about bursting the bubble she'd lived in too long.

"Merry Christmas, Richard."

"Merry Christmas to you too, Regina."

Without saying another word, she whirled around and rushed out of the building like it was caving in. By the time I got outside less than a minute later, she had already made it halfway down the block.

*   *   *

Five minutes past two p.m. I glanced up from my desk and saw Pam standing in my doorway. She walked in and stood by the side of my desk with a blank expression on her face. "How was lunch, Richard?"

"It could have been better. I was supposed to go with Fel, but Sam got hysterical when his computer conked out and I was the only tech around. When I finished with him and made it to the lobby, she had already left, so I went off on my own. I bumped into Regina and one of her coworkers and they invited me to join them. Anyway, I had left Felicia a voice mail before I left the building. I hope she's not too disappointed."

"Pffftt!" Pam rolled her eyes and waved her hands. "It would take a lot to disappoint my girl. I just left her office and she's doing fine."

"I'll give her a call in a few minutes and apologize for standing her up."

"You didn't stand Fel up. Things happen." Pam paused and gave me a guarded look. "By the way, did you know she's thinking about looking for a job in Atlanta?"

My breath caught in my throat. I narrowed my eyes and gawked at Pam. Then the words shot out of my mouth like bullets. "What are you talking about? I didn't even know she was thinking about leaving the company, let alone going to work in Atlanta. She told you that?"

"Uh-huh. Poor thing." Pam sighed and shook her head. "She's getting so bored with the way things are."

"I didn't know Felicia felt that way."

"Who wouldn't? No children, no husband, no pets to keep her company. Her parents might be moving to Atlanta when they get back, so there'd be nothing to keep her here. She's so good at her job and so personable, other companies would hire her on the spot. And the way she was talking, it won't be long before she makes her move."

"Well, whatever she decides to do, I wish her well."

"Me too." Pam leaned forward and glared at me. "Have you given any thought to what I told you?"

I knew what she was talking about, but I asked anyway. "What do you mean?"

"She *loves* you, Richard. And I know it's none of my business, but don't you have feelings for her? And I'm not talking about as just a friend."

"Pam, that's something I don't want to discuss at this time."

She threw up her hands. "Okay. I can tell when I'm overstepping my bounds. I can see it makes you uncomfortable, so I—"

"That's not it, Pam. It's just that, well, I need a little more time to digest what you told me. I'll see you on the bus this evening."

I was glad Pam left when she did. The only person I wanted to discuss what she'd told me was Felicia herself. If what Pam told me was true, and I had no reason not to believe her, either Felicia or I had to make a move eventually. I had a feeling I'd be the one to do it.

I stared at my monitor for a few moments. Then I picked up the phone, but I didn't dial Felicia's number. I decided to go to her office. When I got there, she was busy talking to her clerks in the cubicle they shared. When she looked up and saw me, she held up her hand and pointed toward her office. I slunk in and sat down. She joined me about a minute later.

"What's up, Richard?" She sat down at her desk and gave me an expressionless look.

"I apologize for missing lunch."

"I got your message. You said something came up. . . ." She sounded so detached it was eerie.

"How about having lunch tomorrow?"

"I won't be available. I'm going to take off the rest of the week. We can do it one day next week, but it's not really necessary. I can wrap up the Christmas party plans by myself."

"I see. Well, can we get together for lunch anyway? I'd really like to make it up to you."

"Richard, you don't need to make up anything to me."

"But can I still take you to lunch next week?"

She took her time responding. "Let's wait until next week gets here. If you still want to take me, ask me then."

"Okay. I'll see you on the bus this evening. If I get on before you, I'll make sure and save the seat right beside me like I always do."

"I'm leaving early today, so I won't be on the bus."

"I see. Well, I hope you enjoy your weekend. I'll check with you next week."

"Sure. Thanks for coming by, Richard." She turned around to face her computer and started pecking away. That was my cue to leave.

CHAPTER 19
FELICIA

When I realized Richard was not going to show up after I'd waited twenty minutes for him in the lobby, I'd picked up a shrimp salad from the cafeteria and returned to my office. Before I started eating, I noticed that my landline message-waiting light was blinking. There was only one message and it was from Richard. I was not surprised to hear that he'd skipped lunch with me today because something had come up. I'd lost count of all the times I'd canceled and rescheduled lunch with somebody for the same reason. Now that I knew he had called, I didn't see any reason to call him back right away.

Ten minutes after I'd finished my lunch, Pam walked past my office. The door was open, so she peeped in and did a double take when she saw me sitting at my desk. She rushed in with her mouth hanging open. "Felicia, I thought Richard was taking you to lunch today."

"I thought so too. I waited twenty minutes for him downstairs before I realized he wasn't going to show up. So, I came back up here. He left a voice mail message to let me know that something had come up, though. Probably a last-minute meeting."

Pam sat down and gave me a dry look. "Hmmm. I wonder why he'd be having a 'last-minute meeting' with Regina. . . ." She sniffed and folded her arms.

"Excuse me?"

"I stopped working long enough to run out and grab a sandwich from that deli down the street. I saw Richard escorting Regina into Wing Lu's place next door to the deli."

I shrugged. "So?"

"He broke a lunch date with you to go with her."

"Richard can spend time with whoever he wants." The words tasted like rotting food in my mouth. "Now, can we change the subject?" I didn't give Pam time to answer. "I was dead serious when I told you that I might go work for another firm. I'm going to try and line up some interviews as soon as possible."

"Christmas is right around the corner. This is a bad time to be looking for a new job. Why don't you just wait until after the New Year?"

"I don't think I can wait that long."

Pam stood up with a sad expression on her face. "Well, I hope you're only thinking about leaving. You'll never find another boss like Sam. But no matter what you decide to do, I'm with you all the way," she said in a weary tone. "I'd better get back to my office. I'll see you on the bus this evening."

I had not planned to leave early or take off the rest of the week until this afternoon. I had no right to feel slighted because Richard chose to have lunch with Regina instead of me. But I did. I was spinning out of control and I didn't like it. The most logical thing for me to do was to get over him. That meant seeing less of him. And I would start today by not riding the bus home with him.

I sent an e-mail to Sam to let him know that "for personal reasons" I'd be leaving in a few minutes and I wouldn't return until Monday. On my way out, I stopped by my clerks' workstation to tell them the same thing. I hadn't taken off personal time in ten months, so I didn't feel the least bit guilty.

"Are you feeling okay, Fel?" Ramona asked. "You look fine."

"I'm fine. I just need a little break," I said with a dry laugh. "You all have my cell phone number. Give me a call if you need me. Make sure you collect all the materials after the class ends." I glanced around the hall area. "If you guys want to put up the decorations before I get back, feel free to do so."

"Christmas is still over three weeks away," Marybeth chimed in.

"I know. But a lot of people like to get started early. I've already received a few cards. The folks in personnel and in the payroll department have already put up a few wreaths and streamers. If you guys want to wait until later in the month, that's fine. But we really need to get started on it by the end of next week. I'd hate for people to think that our holiday spirit was low this year." Despite the fact that I was slightly disappointed about Richard not showing up, I was still as excited about Christmas as always. Just thinking about how festive my apartment was going to look when I put up my tree and everything else lifted my spirits. But I still wanted to go home.

When I got to my apartment, I immediately checked my messages. Daddy had called to say that he and Mama were having a ball in Tokyo,

Japan. "Baby, these folks over here are treating us like royalty," he whooped. "If I knew the language, I'd talk your mama into us moving over here for good." Just hearing my daddy's voice made me smile.

Right after I put on a pot of collard greens, I called up Grandma Lucy. "You want to spend a few days over here?" I asked. "I'm going to be off work the rest of the week, so we can get some serious Christmas shopping done."

Grandma Lucy sucked on her teeth before she replied. "Aw, shuck it! I can't. Daisy Hawthorne invited me to go to Atlantic City with her on account of her sister June had to cancel and they can't get a refund on her plane ticket. I done already started packing so her son can drive us to the airport."

"Oh, that's nice. When are you leaving?"

"Tomorrow morning."

"Tomorrow? How come you didn't tell me before now?"

"I didn't know before now. Daisy just asked me to go about a hour ago. I was going to tell you this evening when you got home from work. We'll be gone five or six days. Or did Daisy say seven or eight?"

"Don't forget to pack your pills. And make sure you give me the name of your hotel so I can check up on you every day."

Grandma Lucy laughed. "Why do you need to 'check up' on me every day? I'm a grown woman."

"Give me the name of the hotel anyway," I insisted.

"I will! Humph! You worry more than my mama did when I was growing up." Grandma Lucy let out a loud breath and then softened her tone. "Baby, get a life. *Get yourself a husband* so you won't have so much time on your hands to be fretting over me."

I rolled my eyes and shook my head. "I'll let you go so you can finish your packing."

"Fel, I just want you to be happy."

"I am happy."

"I don't think you can stay that way too much longer by yourself."

"What are you trying to say?"

"I ain't 'trying' to say nothing. I'm saying it: Get married before all your eggs dry up or you won't never know what a blessing being a mama is. Let me go to my grave with a smile on my face."

I couldn't think of anything to say other than "Good night. If I don't see you or talk to you again before you leave, have fun."

Pam called me up from her house a few minutes after six p.m. "What's going on?" Her panicked tone made me panic. I rubbed my tightening chest as she went on. "When I stopped by your office this evening so we could walk to the bus stop together, Sandy told me you'd left early and would be off until Monday! Did you have an emergency?" She paused and lowered her voice. "Or is this because I told you I saw Richard having lunch with Regina today?"

"No, I was just feeling kind of blah. So I decided to take a break and refresh myself," I explained.

"Why?"

"Because I have a few things to sort out in the next few weeks."

"Are you still thinking about leaving the company?"

"Yes, I am."

A moment of silence passed before Pam went on. "I'm worried about you, girl. I'm going to have Clyde come get you and take you to a movie or something tonight. I'm trying to get his mind off that heifer in Cleveland."

"Don't you dare send him over here! If he wants to have a relationship with that 'heifer' in Cleveland, I don't want to interfere."

"Then I'll send him over to bring you a plate so you won't have to cook this evening. He's just waking up from his nap. Let me ask him."

Before I could stop her, I heard mumbling on her end and a few seconds later, Clyde was on the phone. "Hey, Fel. I ain't doing nothing until later tonight. Do you want me to come over and bring you a bucket of chicken or something?"

"No, you don't have to do that. I'm cooking some collard greens."

"Is that right? Well, if you ain't expecting company, do you mind if I come over and eat dinner with you?"

"Clyde, I have a lot of things to do this evening and I don't really feel like having company."

"I can't even come get them greens?"

"Not tonight. I'm cooking a small bunch anyway. I'll be cooking some again soon and you can come over then."

"All right, then. Whenever that is, I just hope I'll be available. . . ."

Right after I got out of bed Saturday morning, I realized it was the first day of December, which always put me in a more festive mood. When I was a little girl, this was the day I'd start crossing off the days toward the countdown to Christmas.

I spent most of the day shopping and at the movie theater a mile from my apartment. It had been a while since I'd seen a good movie, so I watched *Crazy Rich Asians* twice.

When I got up Sunday morning, I called the

same elderly church members I had left messages for. None of them needed my assistance anytime soon, but each one was pleased when I promised to give them another call in a week or so.

I had planned to go to church because Pastor Barkley always made a special Christmas speech every year on the first Sunday in December. But the next thing I knew, the wind was howling so hard, my windows rattled. And the sky was so dark, it looked like a gray tarp. Those dreary things made me change my mind about going out at all. After enjoying a plate of grits, bacon, eggs, and toast, I made out checks for my rent and a few other monthly bills, accepted an invitation to participate in a cancer walk-a-thon in February, and left a few posts on Facebook and Twitter. I spent the next few hours reading and watching three episodes of *Shaka Zulu* on Netflix.

Grandma Lucy had called me up Thursday evening to let me know they'd made it to Atlantic City. And we had spoken for a few minutes on Friday. We had not communicated on Saturday, so I decided to give her a call before I got ready for bed Sunday night. I was stunned when the hotel operator told me she'd checked out Saturday morning. I immediately dialed her home phone number. She answered on the second ring. "What are you doing home?" I asked, almost out of breath.

"I live here, that's why," she said in a casual tone.

"You just left here on Thursday. I thought you were going to be gone five or six—or seven or eight days?"

"I thought I was too. When Daisy lost all her money Saturday morning fiddling around with that roulette wheel, she didn't want to stay no longer. So we checked out and hopped on the next plane to Cleveland. She forgot to get in touch with her son to let him know we was coming home early, so he wasn't at the airport to pick us up."

"How did you get home?"

"I took a cab."

"Why didn't you call me?"

Grandma Lucy ignored my question and abruptly changed the subject. "I had a ball flouncing around in them fancy casinos. Me and Daisy ate like hogs and we slept in a suite fit for a movie star. On top of all that, I won a bunch of money. What did you do while I was gone?"

"Um . . . nothing worth mentioning."

"That's what I figured."

CHAPTER 20
FELICIA

After my conversation with Grandma Lucy, I took my trash to the dumpster. I had on my coat and boots, but it was so cold and windy, by the time I got back to the lobby, my hands were so stiff I could barely bend my fingers. Our elevator was so slow, it could take a couple of minutes for it to travel from one floor to another. I waited three minutes before I decided to take the stairs. I planned to take care of a lot of chores today. Before I could get back inside my apartment, Lorena opened her door.

"I bought some eggnog this morning!" she yelled. "You want to come over for some? The Wilsons from down the hall might stop by later."

"I don't think so. I drank a couple of glasses of cider a little while ago."

"Then come over for a few minutes so we can chat. I knocked on your door yesterday and the day before and you didn't answer. Where were you?"

"I didn't hear you. I must have been in the shower, or straightening up my back bedroom."

"Next time I'll call first. Anyway, I was getting worried about you. You in there by yourself and all." Lorena gave me a concerned look and lowered her voice. "It's not healthy for you to spend too much time alone, especially this time of year. It could lead to depression."

"I'm not depressed," I protested.

"And I don't want you to be. It can make you do things you'll regret." Lorena motioned for me to enter her apartment. I reluctantly followed her to the kitchen and flopped down in a chair at her cluttered table. She poured me a huge glass of eggnog anyway.

"Like I was saying, depression can make people do things they'll regret."

I took a long pull from my glass. "Like go on a shopping spree to cheer themselves up?"

"Worse. Whenever I get in a lackluster mood, I can call up one of my exes and invite them over."

I snickered. "If he's an ex, something went wrong and he may not want to see you."

"Uh-uh. I only call up the ones that I ended the relationship with."

I chuckled and waved my hand. "My exes are so far in the past, I doubt if any of them still remember me."

Lorena gave me a pitiful look. "Felicia, you need to be with that man—whoever he is—that you saw with another woman at Ralph's Market Black Friday evening. The one you're in love with. Otherwise, this thing is going to eat away at you until you lose your perspective."

"Like I already told you, I can only admire him from afar. I doubt if that's ever going to change." I finished my eggnog and left.

I was glad when Monday morning rolled around so I could go back to work. I wasn't ready to get back on the bus and face Richard yet, though. Or Pam, for that matter, because I knew she was going to drill me like a bad tooth the next time I saw her. I tried not to spend too much time thinking about Richard. But it seemed like the harder I tried, the more I thought about him. I couldn't believe the position I was in. Being in love with him was like being in love with a movie star; both were unreachable. I'd miss him if he accepted that position in the home office, and/or if I left the company and relocated. Whatever happened, I was going to learn to live with it.

I reluctantly decided to drive to work. It didn't take long for me to regret making that decision. Traffic was so heavy, I scolded myself for not calling Uber or taking a later bus. If I had, I could have at least kicked back and taken a nap or gotten some reading done.

When I finally made it to my destination, the parking garage in our building had no more spaces available. I ended up parking in a lot six blocks away. There was a thick blanket of fresh snow on the ground and patches of ice all over the place. Within minutes after I'd started walking, I saw three people slip and fall. When I almost went down myself, I flagged down a taxi.

Pam waltzed into my office a few minutes past nine thirty.

"I'm so glad to see you. I left you two voice mails on Saturday and sent a text on Sunday," she wailed, sitting down.

"I'm sorry I didn't get back to you. I was busy all weekend."

"I figured that's what it was. I'm sure you'll be glad when your mama gets home so she can help you keep your grandmother occupied."

"My grandmother went to Atlantic City with

one of her friends. She left on Thursday and got back yesterday."

"That Miss Lucy. She sure gets around. I hope I'll be as frisky as she is when I reach her age." Pam pursed her lips and gazed at me. "Richard has asked me several times since last Thursday if I'd heard from you. He was worried."

Her last sentence threw me for a loop. "He was worried about me?"

"Yup. Almost as much as I was. But I'm glad everything's all right." She stood up and stretched. "There is so much work on my desk. I'd better get back to my office. I might come back later for coffee."

Ten minutes after Pam left, Richard walked into my office. "How's it going?" he asked. I hoped he wouldn't sit down. I was surprised to see him in a turtleneck sweater the same color as the one I had on today, with a similar design. We both wore black slacks. Was our "matching ensemble" fate? I wondered.

"Everything is fine, Richard."

"Hey, that's a sharp outfit you have on."

"So is yours." We laughed. "How was your weekend?"

He slapped his forehead with the palm of his hand. "Chaotic. My girls ran me ragged: a volleyball game, lunch, and shopping at the mall. You name it, we did it. I barely had time to catch my breath."

"Yeah, I was quite busy myself."

"So . . ." He rubbed his hands together and paused. "Are you available for lunch today? I really would like to take you."

"Let me think about it," I said in a stiff tone.

"Okay. It would mean a lot to me. . . ." He sounded so sincere and mysterious I didn't know what to think.

If having lunch with me meant so much to him, I had to give it a little more consideration. "I think I'm available today," I said coyly. "What time would you like to go?"

"Noon. I'll meet you in your office this time. And I promise I won't let Sam hold me up like he did last Wednesday."

That was not something I expected to hear. "You were with Sam?" It was on the tip of my tongue to tell him that Pam had told me she'd seen him having lunch with Regina. I had no idea why he was lying to me. Maybe he wasn't the upstanding, wholesome man I thought he was after all.

"Just as I was about to leave my office, he came flying in in a panic. He was having computer issues and didn't want to lose some important information. You know how long-winded he is, so by the time I was able to get away from him, you'd left. Anyway, I had no idea where you were. I was at loose ends until I ran into Regina. She talked me into going for dim sum at Wing Lu's with her and one of her coworkers."

"Oh." So he hadn't stood me up or lied. I felt so much better. "I'm fine with meeting you in the lobby. No need to swing by my office."

He smiled and said, "Okay, I'll see you at noon."

CHAPTER 21

RICHARD

When I got to the lobby fifteen minutes before noon, I was pleased to see a gigantic Christmas tree in the middle of the floor with dozens of gift-wrapped boxes stacked underneath it. A blow-up Santa Claus stood a few feet from the entrance. Fake snow had been sprinkled in various spots on the floor. If Felicia didn't show up at noon, I was prepared to wait at least another twenty or thirty minutes. When she strolled out of the elevator at exactly noon, she rushed up to me. That put a huge smile on my face.

"Are we still going to Andre's?" she asked with a smile almost as wide as mine.

"There or anyplace you'd like," I suggested.

She glanced out the window and frowned. "It's so nasty outside. Can we pick up something from the cafeteria and find an empty conference room?"

"That's not a bad idea. But I'd like to take you to a nice place to make up for last Wednesday."

"Richard, I told you to forget about that. It's not that important. I've been stood up before."

Her last remark gave me a start, but it was understandable. "I'd still like to take you to Andre's Bistro or another nice place."

She took her time responding. "Okay. Let's concentrate on today for now."

We picked up sandwiches and drinks from the cafeteria, and went to a conference room on the third floor where Sam conducted some of his meetings.

There were more than thirty empty seats around the oblong-shaped table, but I chose one right beside her. "Before we start discussing our Christmas event, I wanted you to update me on your parents' globe-trotting activities. What city are they in now?" I asked as we unwrapped our sandwiches.

Her eyes lit up and her voice sounded softer when she answered. "Tokyo, Japan. And they are having a ball."

"That's an amazing city. Thanks to Uncle Sam, I got to visit it when I was in the army." I bit off a piece of my sandwich. I chewed and swallowed it as fast as I could. She did the same. "I know you mentioned that they'd started planning and saving for their epic journey thirty-five or forty years ago. What was it that made them choose the specific countries on their itinerary?"

"Well, like most African Americans, my family has roots in Africa and Europe. When they started showing those TV ads about DNA ancestry testing, my parents immediately jumped on that. When they received their pie charts, they were amazed."

"How so?"

"We couldn't believe we had no Native American blood. And Daddy was stunned to find out he's one-eighth Japanese. Anyway, they met with their travel agent earlier this year and selected various cities in each country on their charts. They decided to spend from a few days to a couple of weeks, or longer, in each one. The last location on their list is the Holy Land. That's kind of tentative right now because the only hotel their travel agent has been able to reserve so far is in a remote area where some people still live in tents."

"Really? Did their DNA ancestry charts include that region too?"

"No, but they've always been eager to see what it's really like."

"That is so interesting. How come you didn't want to go with them?"

"I didn't even consider it. This was their time to be alone. They both have a few minor health issues, so they couldn't put it off too much longer. But I plan to visit a lot of the same places someday. I'd love to know more about the locations and ethnicities involved in my DNA. We traveled a lot as a family when I was growing up, though. One year we went to Hawaii twice. The following year it was Mexico and the Bahamas. I'm from a very adventurous family." Felicia was beaming like a lamp by now. I enjoyed hearing more about her personal life.

"Fantastic. I am so impressed. I wish my folks had lived long enough to fulfill more of their dreams." I suddenly felt a twinge of sadness, but I kept my voice upbeat. "My parents had a hard life. For the most part they were happy, though. And let me tell you, they kept my brother and me on a tight leash." I chuckled. "Both my parents worked for the post office. Dad was also a Baptist minister and you know how preachers and parents in other power positions make their kids toe the line."

"Tell me about it. My mother was a nurse, so she monitored the health of everybody in our family. If my brother and I sneezed or coughed more than one time in the same day, she'd make us take pills and go to bed. My father was a homicide detective, so he thought a lot of young people were potential suspects. We never even looked at the wild crowd, let along hang out with them." Felicia took a deep breath and a wistful look crossed her face. "When I was eight, my mother took me to work with her one day. She introduced me to some of her patients, but the one I'll never forget was a little girl around six. She had brain cancer and had only months to live. I felt so guilty about being in good health and having such a wonderful life. That weekend when my father gave me my allowance, which was only five dollars, I donated it to the cancer foundation. For the next few months, every single week I donated half of my allowance to them. When I finished college and started working, I increased the amount and every time Sam gives me a raise, I increase it even more."

"What a coincidence. I've been making monthly donations to three of my favorite charities since I started working too. So do my girls—and you know how teenagers like to spend money on themselves and their friends. But last year when Carol's grandfather gave her a crisp one-hundred-dollar bill for her birthday, she donated it all to St. Jude Children's Research Hospital after watching one of their TV commercials."

"You must be very proud of your children."

"I am. They're my world." I swallowed a lump that had suddenly formed in my throat. "You know something, Felicia, the more I learn about you, the more I'm intrigued. Even with all the stories we've shared over the years, I feel like there's so much more to appreciate. I love . . . talking with you."

Felicia gazed at me for a few seconds, her silence making me wonder if I'd given away my growing feelings for her. Finally, she said, "My grandmother likes to say, 'Still waters run deep.' " We laughed. "Okay, we don't have much time, so let's move on to the real reason we got together today." We laughed again. "The first thing I want to discuss is the location of our Christmas event."

I wanted to continue talking about personal things. With all the driving I'd done recently, I'd missed out on our commuter bus conversations. "Oh yeah, the location. I mentioned that to Sam this morning. He thinks we should have it in the cafeteria. And he wants it to happen no later than the week before Christmas so the eighteenth is the date we're going with."

"After regular business hours?" she asked with her brows furrowed.

"That won't work because several folks have already told him that they probably won't attend unless it's during the lunch hour. And I don't blame them. Who knows what the weather will be like that day. Last year it was so bad half of the businesses on this block shut down for a few days."

"I remember. And it seems like Ohio winters get a little more severe each year. I envy the folks who live in the South."

"Speaking of the South, Pam said you're considering job opportunities in Atlanta."

Felicia took a sip of her iced tea and nibbled on her sandwich for a few seconds. "I did some Internet searches and it sounds like the place to be these days." After another sip, she exhaled and shifted in her seat. "Now let's get back to the Christmas plans. The more I think about having a gift exchange like you suggested, I don't think that's a good idea. We're talking about dozens of folks and a gift exchange could take up a lot of time. The cafeteria folks only allow up to two and a half hours for special events.

"Hmmm. I hadn't thought about the time frame. Well, let's deep-six the gift exchange. What about a deejay?"

"Richard, we don't have to worry about that. The cafeteria always provides recorded Christmas music the last two weeks in the year. And one of the cooks told me they'd be putting up a tree, garlands, wreaths, and everything else next week, so we won't have to deal with that chore either."

"Good!" I rubbed my palms together and

winked at Felicia. "The only thing left is the menu."

"And the head count," she pointed out. "I'll get that when I send out a group e-mail in a day or so. I'll get some selection choices from the cafeteria folks and include that information in the e-mail so the attendees can help us pick the menu. If you can think of anything else, give me a call or send me an e-mail." She turned to retrieve her purse from the back of her chair.

"Do you have to leave now?" When I placed my hand on top of hers, she contemplated our joined hands for a few moments.

"Not really. I was just going to go back to my office and read the newspaper." She gently pulled her hand away.

"We still have a few minutes left. If you don't mind, can we talk a little longer?"

Felicia shifted in her seat again. "What about?"

"Well, your interest in relocating to Atlanta. Won't you miss your family?"

I didn't know what to make of the guarded look that suddenly appeared on her face. "My brother lives in Atlanta. My parents and my grandmother might move there to be closer to him and his family when my parents get back. These Ohio winters have finally taken a toll on them—and me. If they do move, there won't be anything to keep me here." She paused and a pensive look crossed her face. "By the way, I heard that the folks in the home office want you to come work with them."

"Yeah, that." I scratched my chin and shook my head. "It is tempting, but I'm going to pass on it."

"Oh? Why is that, if you don't mind sharing?"

"You see, every decision I make affects my girls. I haven't even told them about the offer. But they've made it clear that they'd never want to leave this place."

"I guess being single is not so bad after all. I can pack up and take off at the drop of a hat. Besides, I've put off buying a house long enough and I'm ready to settle down. Forty is creeping up on me."

"Tell me about it. Forty caught up with me last March." We laughed again. "You know, I never thought I'd still be single at this age."

"I never thought I'd still be single either," she mumbled with a faraway look in her eyes.

I cleared my throat. The next thing I said flew out of my mouth before I could stop it. "I won't be single too much longer, though."

Felicia took a deep breath and blinked. I couldn't believe how mournful she suddenly looked. Well, she was a sensitive woman, so that didn't really surprise me. A few years ago, she'd actually cried at a going-away office gathering when one of the clerks she'd trained resigned. "You're getting married?" I couldn't tell if she was making a statement or asking a question. "That's wonderful. I hope I'm still around when it happens."

"I'm sure you will be. I'm going to move things along very quickly. As a matter of fact, I hope you can do me a big favor."

"What kind of favor?" She sounded as meek as a newborn kitten.

"You know I've always admired your taste. You have a beautiful wardrobe. And excluding Michelle Obama and Oprah, I've never seen another woman wear jewelry as stunning as yours."

"Thanks, Richard. I appreciate the compliments."

"When it comes to picking out jewelry, you're the best. My mother-in-law wears the earrings you helped me pick out more than any other pair. And the bracelet you helped me choose for my daughter's birthday, she likes it so much she made me buy another one exactly like it in case she loses the first one."

"Oh really?" She looked at me with a large grin splitting her face. "I'm glad to hear that. I enjoy shopping for other folks almost as much as I enjoy shopping for myself. If you want me to help you pick out something else, just let me know."

"That's the favor. Would you mind accompanying me to Wallace Jewelers again? We can go at lunchtime. I need to pick out an engagement ring and I'd sure like your input."

Felicia gawked at me as if I'd just turned into a gremlin. She blinked rapidly a few times and then took a deep breath. "You want me to help you pick out an . . . engagement ring?" After a brief pause, she got real giddy. "Of course! I'm glad you think my taste is that good. But picking out an item that important is serious. It's not something I'd want to do on a lunch hour. I'd like to take my time and Wallace Jewelers stays open until eight."

"In that case, I'll drive in the day we decide to go so I can give you a ride home afterward. Um . . ." I paused and scratched the side of my head. "I'd appreciate it if you'd keep this to yourself in case I get cold feet."

"Of course," she muttered.

"One more thing. I'd like to take you to dinner that evening for doing me this favor."

"Okay. I'd like that. When would you like to go?"

"If you don't have any plans for this Friday, will that work for you? My girls are going to a slumber party next door that night, so I won't have to rush home that evening."

"Sure. Friday works for me." She checked the time. "Listen, I have a ton of e-mails to reply to, so I'm going to head back to my office."

We rose at the same time. "I'm glad we were able to get together today. I wish I could have offered more input for the holiday luncheon."

"You did enough, Richard. And to be honest with you, I could have finished this on my own, or with Pam. But I'm glad you helped." We headed toward the exit. "I drove in today, so I think I'll sneak out a little early so I can beat some of that traffic."

"Will you be on the bus tomorrow morning?"

"As far as I know."

"Then unless I run into you before you leave today, I'll see you then."

My office was on the same floor in the opposite direction, but I walked her to the elevator. Felicia pressed the down button, and there was a very awkward moment of silence. I stared at the wall, she stared at the floor. When she suddenly looked up she said, "Richard, I'm very happy for you. I wish you all the luck in the world with your upcoming nuptials. I'm sure you'll be very happy."

"I know I will," I replied.

CHAPTER 22
RICHARD

"You two better behave at Mrs. Randolph's house tonight," I warned my girls Friday morning. I was driving in to work, so they would get a ride to school this morning. We had just finished washing the breakfast dishes and were preparing to leave. "I'll be calling over there throughout the night."

"Why?" Marva asked with her eyes opened so wide she resembled a gecko.

"To make sure everything is going okay," I answered. Both girls huffed out exasperated sighs as they followed me to the coatrack in the living room.

"Daddy, don't you have more important things

to do with your time on a Friday night?" Marva asked. "Like going on a date!"

"And instead of calling to check up on us, why don't you just come over there? I know Mrs. Randolph would like that," Carol teased.

I buttoned my coat before I responded. "I have news for you two, I'm going out to dinner after work today."

"With who?" they asked at the same time.

"A very special lady."

Marva and Carol glanced at each other with their mouths hanging open and then they looked at me. "The same one you went to lunch with last Wednesday?" Carol asked with a self-satisfied smirk.

"We didn't make it to lunch that day. But she's the same lady. We decided to go have dinner instead."

"Oh well. I hope she keeps your attention enough so you won't have to call and check up on us every hour," Carol said hopefully.

"Bundle up, grab those backpacks, and let's get up out of here," I ordered as I ushered them to the garage.

I dropped the girls off in front of their school and headed toward the freeway. On the way, I saw several compact cars parked on the street

that were almost completely covered in snow.
The vehicles that were moving were creeping
along at such a slow pace, I was tempted to take
my SUV back home and catch the bus after all.
If I hadn't told Felicia we could go to the jewelry
store after work and that I would drive her
home, I would have.

I had spent a lot of time last night wondering
what went through her mind when I told her I
was going to propose to someone. I was glad she
didn't ask the name of my "fiancée" because I
don't know how I would have wiggled out of
that. But I had to ask myself if I had lost my
mind. Here I was about to do either the stupid-
est thing I'd ever done, or the smartest. I be-
lieved what Pam had told me: Felicia was in love
with me. However, I wondered if she loved me
enough to want to be my wife. I'd come too far
to turn back, so I was going to ask her to marry
me. I just didn't know when—it had to be before
she left the company—and I didn't know how.
I'd proposed to Regina over dinner. And I'd
done the same thing with Margaret. I wanted
this proposal to be more original. I couldn't wait
to see Felicia's face when I presented her with
the engagement ring that she'd helped me pick
out for my fiancée.

On the way to my office, I picked up a cup of

coffee from the cafeteria. Pam accosted me when I got off the elevator. "Well now," she said, looking at her watch. "I was beginning to think you weren't coming in." She pursed her lips and gave me a suspicious look. "What are you up to these days? Anything new with you?" If that wasn't a leading question I didn't know what was. Even though I had asked Felicia to keep the ring-buying business to herself, I suspected she'd told Pam anyway. With Pam knowing she was in love with me, there was just no telling what was going through her mind.

I didn't stop walking as I replied, "Same old routine."

When lunchtime rolled around, I asked one of the other technicians to bring me a sandwich. I hadn't left my office since I'd come in. The reason for that was I didn't want to see Felicia before evening because I was afraid I'd lose my nerve. However, even if I did buy a ring, I could still back out and she'd never know what I'd been up to.

Throughout the afternoon, Pam walked past my office several times, giving me the same suspicious look she'd given me earlier. Each time I was on the telephone or had someone in my office, which was probably why she didn't come in and start up again.

I finally called up Felicia at three fifteen. She answered on the first ring. "Hello, Richard. Are we still on for this evening?"

"I hope so. Do you want to go eat dinner before we go to the jewelry store?"

"If you don't mind, let's skip that. I had a super burrito for lunch, so I don't think I'll be hungry again for a while. Besides that, my grandmother is spending a few days with me and she just called and told me she's cooking dinner this evening. When my granny cooks for me, I never leave the table until I've eaten everything on my plate. Otherwise, she'd be offended and would pout like a two-year-old." We laughed.

"I see. Well, I hope you'll still let me give you a ride home. I'd hate for you to be out there waiting on a bus. And, if it's okay with you, I sure would like to come in and say hello to Sister Lucy. I haven't seen her since last spring when my girls and I ran into you and her at Macy's."

"And that's a day to remember. She'd been looking for a hat to wear to church on Easter. When you saw us, we'd already been to eight other hat stores."

"Did she ever find one she liked?"

"In the first store we'd gone to." We laughed again. "Okay, I'll be ready to go at five, so why don't we meet in the lobby then."

"I'll see you there."

*   *   *

There was only one other customer in the jewelry store when we got there, and he was on his way out.

"The snow must really be coming down now. You two look like snowmen!" the sharp-nosed woman behind the counter remarked.

"I feel like one too," Felicia said.

"How can I help you folks today?" The clerk scanned our faces with an anxious look I had become so familiar with. It was no wonder, she was the same middle-aged blonde who had waited on me the other two times Felicia helped me pick out jewelry. Her name was Clarice.

"I'd like to look at engagement rings today," I replied.

"Oh! Well, you've come to the right place!" Clarice blinked at Felicia and grinned. "I hope we have something to your liking, my dear."

"I came to help my friend choose something for his fiancée," Felicia said quickly as she shifted her weight from one foot to the other. She was good at hiding her emotions, but I noticed a slightly sad look on her face. That made me feel guilty. I had no idea how long she'd been in love with me. For her to hear that I was going to get married must have crushed her. She wouldn't feel that way much longer.

"What price range do you have in mind?" Clarice asked, looking directly at me.

When I told her, she pointed to a display in the case in front of us. "Do you know your future bride's ring size?"

I gazed at Felicia's hand. "About the same as yours, Fel."

Her jaw dropped. "I wouldn't know," she said sharply.

"I'm sure you're the same size." I cleared my throat and gave her a thoughtful look. "Ma'am, can we take a look at the second tray to the right?"

"Absolutely!" With an amused look on her face now, Clarice eagerly removed the tray from the case and set it on the counter. It contained six rings; all were stunning. I passed up the first two and removed the third one.

"What do you think, Fel? Is this something you'd select for yourself?"

"No." She sniffed and pointed to the ring at the end of the tray. "I like that one," she said with a wistful expression on her face as she admired the ring.

"Great choice!" Clarice was probably so giddy because Felicia had picked the most eye-catching ring in the bunch. "Our two-carat, white gold, oval-cut halo is very popular."

It was a great choice. "Fel, do you mind trying

it on?" I didn't wait for her answer. I slipped it onto her finger. It was a perfect fit. "That's nice."

"It's gorgeous," Felicia said in a low tone. I held her hand up and stared at it for about eight seconds.

"We have a few more in your price range," Clarice said. "One moment, please." She dashed to a back room and returned less than a minute later with another tray, one with twice as many rings. Felicia spent the next twenty minutes inspecting each one. When she finally chose one, it was the first ring she had liked.

I winked at Clarice. "I'll take this one."

"Mr. Grimes, are you sure? You don't want to look at any others, or go home and think about it? You're spending a lot of money, so I want you to be sure."

"I'm sure," I said firmly. "Please charge it to my account."

Felicia and I didn't speak again until we left the store. When we got outside, I placed my arm around her shoulder and steered her to our office parking garage. "Thanks for helping me out again. You don't know how much this means to me."

"Thanks. I'm glad I could help you again. But I have to say, I don't think there are too many men who'd ask another woman to choose a ring for their fiancée." She chuckled. "This was fun and I'm glad you asked me."

"Well, I'm not that good at selecting things for anybody other than myself. You wouldn't believe how many times my girls, and almost everybody else in my family, have made me return something because it was not to their liking."

"My grandmother is the same way. You could offer her the Hope Diamond and she'd prefer something you'd pick up at a carnival."

I guffawed and tightened my arm around her shoulder. She felt so good. "Looking at the street, I have a feeling it's going to be a rough ride home."

"You're right. Uh, Richard, I know it's none of my business, but are you marrying Regina Dobbins? You don't have to answer that if you don't want to."

"No, I'm not marrying Regina. You and everybody else will meet her soon. . . ."

CHAPTER 23
FELICIA

Within minutes after Richard pulled out of the garage and turned the first corner, we encountered a three-car accident at the end of the block. Emergency vehicles were all over the place and the snow was coming down so hard, it was frightening. "I wasn't expecting this," he commented as he made a U-turn and drove in the opposite direction.

"I hope that accident is not too serious and nobody got hurt," I said.

"I hope not either. Unfortunately, this is what we'll have to deal with until the weather breaks. I hope—" Richard stopped talking when he realized the street we were on had been closed at the second intersection. He made another U-turn. "I'm sorry, Fel. Maybe driving in today wasn't such a great idea after all. I'll get you home as soon as possible, though."

"Richard, I'm not in a hurry, so you don't have to worry about rushing. Just take your time and we'll get to my place when we get there. Besides, I love looking at all the Christmas decorations." I was glad to see that most of the businesses along the way had decorated their buildings with extravagant displays of colored lights, and the usual array of decorations. Our Community Help Center had a sleigh with Santa Claus and eight reindeer on their rooftop. The display that really tugged at my heartstrings was one of the nativity scene on the porch of a restaurant, complete with three wise men kneeling over baby Jesus.

For the first few miles, which included two more detours, we discussed work and a few other unrelated things. Whenever there was a lull in the conversation, I purposely brought up other things to talk about. I made sure they were not close to the subject of the ring and Richard's upcoming nuptials. "I didn't realize until I looked at my calendar before I left home that today is the anniversary of the Pearl Harbor bombing," I said.

"My grandfather was in the navy and was stationed there at the time," he replied. "The military lost a lot of good men that day."

"Was your grandfather one of the casualties?" A split second after I'd asked that question, I realized how stupid it was.

"No," Richard said, grinning. "Otherwise, neither I nor my father would have been conceived."

"That's for sure. I apologize for asking such a bonehead question."

"That's okay. I ask a lot of bonehead questions myself."

"You know, since the weather is so nasty you can just drop me off in front of my building so you can go home and get out of this mess."

"I'm in no hurry myself. I'd still like to spend a little time with that colorful grandmother of yours."

"Okay. Well, I'd better call and let her know I'm bringing company home." I fished my cellphone out of my purse and dialed. Grandma Lucy didn't pick up by the sixth ring, so I hung up and dialed again. "Sometimes she's not close enough to the phone to get to it in time," I explained as I hit the redial button. This time she answered on the first ring.

My grandmother rarely bothered to say hello anymore. "Where you at?" was how she greeted me.

"I'm on my way home. A lot of the streets are closed, so I'm not sure when I'll get there."

"You be careful on that bus. I hope you ain't sitting too close to the door."

"I'm with a friend from work. He drove in today and offered to give me a ride home. I'll bring him in to meet you."

"All right, baby. I hope he can stay for dinner because I been cooking up a storm all day. Them collard greens and that rump roast on the stove is screaming."

"Great. I'll see you soon." I ended the call and we started talking about mundane things again.

We were less than a mile from my apartment building when he brought up the ring. "You know, the ring you chose resembles the one my mother had."

"Oh really? That's interesting." I cleared my throat and steered the conversation in another direction. "I'd better let you know now that my grandmother is going to badger you to stay for dinner. And if you do, she's going to talk your ear off and ask you everything there is to know about you since the day you were born. You can leave at any time. I'm sure you'd rather be doing something else."

Richard glanced at me. "No, I wouldn't."

We remained silent the rest of the way. That gave me time to recall the conversation I'd had with Pam on Monday about Richard asking me to help him select an engagement ring. "And you agreed to do it?" she'd hollered, standing in my office looking at me as if I'd lost my mind.

"Why not? I helped him choose things for his daughter and his mother-in-law."

"Not an engagement ring!"

"Pam, the man is in love with a woman he wants to marry. I think it's wonderful."

"You're happy that the man you're in love with is going to marry another woman?"

"Yes, I am. I want the people I care about to be happy. I'm sure that whenever I do get married, if Richard and I are still in contact, he'll feel the same way for me."

"Well, we made it," Richard said, bringing me back to the present. He parked in front of my building.

The snow had completely covered the sidewalk and the front walkway to my building. As we waded through snow that literally came up to my knees, I noticed Lorena peeping out her front window. When Richard and I reached my front door, she cracked hers open and peeped some more. "Grandma Lucy, I'm home," I yelled when we got inside. "She moves kind of slow," I whispered to Richard as I waved him to my living room couch.

Before he even removed his coat, he pulled

out his cellphone. "I'd better check in with the girls."

While he was talking to his daughters, I dashed toward my guest bedroom. Grandma Lucy was stretched out on the bed watching *Dr. Phil.* "You okay?" I rushed over and gave her a hug and a peck on her cheek.

"I'm fine." She scrambled off the bed and stretched. "I wonder where Dr. Phil finds so many strange people."

Richard was still on his phone, but I lowered my voice anyway. "Come out and meet my friend. Don't get too nosy and don't go overboard trying to get him to stay for dinner."

Grandma Lucy rolled her eyes and gave me a dismissive wave. Then she glanced around the room. "You seen where I left my teeth at?"

"They're in your mouth. Please keep them there until my company leaves," I pleaded with my hands upward in a prayer position. I whirled around and returned to the living room. Richard had ended his call and hung his coat on the rack by the door. "My grandmother will be right out. Are your girls doing okay?"

"Oh, they're in their element." He leaned back on the couch and crossed his legs. "I don't allow them to sleep over too often and when I do, it's a major event for them."

I didn't want to sit down and get comfortable

until Grandma Lucy made her entrance. I stood a few feet from the end of the couch. "Do they know that you're going to get married?" I asked shyly.

Richard shook his head. "Not yet. But I'm sure they'll be happy when I tell them." He stopped talking and uncrossed his legs and a somber look appeared on his face. "The Christmas after my wife passed, the first item on their long wish list was a new mom. That's the only thing that's been on their lists every year since. And it's still the first item."

"That's sweet. I hope your fiancée lives up to their expectations," I commented, hoping I didn't sound the least bit jealous. That was the last thing I wanted Richard to think. I was thankful that something had finally brought me back to my senses enough to end my years-long fascination with him. This turn of events was a bittersweet ending I would never forget. "Well, I'm glad they're finally going to get what they want." Now would have been a good time to ask Richard the identity of his mystery woman. I was surprised he hadn't told me yet, but I didn't want to know right now anyway. This was probably the only occasion when I'd spend so much time alone with him and I wanted to savor it. Having fond memories of him after he'd changed his marital status would help me move on with my life and direct my feelings toward someone else. "In the meantime, can I get you something warm to drink? Cocoa, tea?"

"I'm fine, Felicia." He glanced at his watch.

Just then, Grandma Lucy waltzed into the room smoothing down the sides of her plaid housedress. As soon as she spotted Richard, she started grinning. She grinned even harder when I introduced him. She sat down next to him and I flopped down into the wing chair facing the couch. "Sister Lucy, I hope you don't mind my coming over at such short notice."

"Son, we love having company. And the more the merrier," Grandma Lucy gushed.

"Thank you. I promise I won't be any trouble, ma'am."

"Richard, the roads are so hazardous, you might be here a while," I pointed out.

"I guess I should get another weather up-date." He pulled out his cellphone again. After staring at the screen for a few moments, he frowned. "This is worse than I thought. According to a report that was posted two minutes ago, most of the streets leading from here to mine have been temporarily closed. It could be several hours before the street cleaners clear them off."

"Well, stay here until they do," I suggested.

He shook his head and put his phone back

into his pocket. "I don't want to be in the way," he protested, rather weakly I noticed.

"Now you listen here, young man, we'd rather have you 'be in the way' than go out there and wreck," Grandma snarled as she wagged her finger in Richard's face. "I'd hate to read about you in the newspaper."

"I appreciate the invitation—"

"Hush up. This ain't no invitation. This is common sense. Fel, you got plenty of clean blankets and pillows." Grandma Lucy shot me an amused look. "After we eat, you make up a pallet on the couch for this boy. I'll go put dinner on the table."

It was a tense but quick meal. As much as I loved collard greens and rump roast, and as hungry as I was by now, I had to force myself to eat the mountain of food Grandma Lucy had set in front of me. She and Richard had no trouble gobbling up everything on their plates, though.

After dinner and a lot of small talk about nothing significant, we returned to the living room. I immediately excused myself to go change out of my work clothes. I didn't want to take too long because I didn't want my grandmother to say anything inappropriate to Richard. I was out of the room only a few minutes, but it was a few minutes too long.

When I returned, Grandma Lucy wobbled up

off the couch and ran up to me with her arms waving like a windmill. "I knew it, I knew it! I been having a feeling all day! *This is the man you're going to marry!*" she boomed, hugging me so hard I could barely breathe.

When I started squirming, she released me. I felt so light-headed I thought I was going to pass out. I gave Richard an apologetic look. "No, Grandma Lucy. He's engaged to marry some-one else."

"No, he ain't. My head ain't just a wig-hat stand. I got a sharp brain. When you told me that time you had a 'special friend,' I knew what that meant. He just told me he was your 'special friend' and when he showed me the engage-ment ring you helped him pick out this evening, I put two and two together!"

I sat back down and gave Richard a weak smile. "I'm sorry. She gets confused a lot."

Richard gazed at me a long time before he re-sponded. "She's not confused this time," he said, rising. The next thing I knew, he pulled the ring case out of his pocket and strolled over to me.

"Huh?" I almost hit the floor when he opened the case and held it up to my face.

"Felicia, will you marry me?"

I knew Richard had a sense of humor, but this

was not funny. "Richard, don't joke about something so serious."

"I'm not joking," he said with so much emphasis, I knew he was serious.

My whole body felt numb, especially my mouth. "What . . . what about the other woman?" I asked when I was able to speak again.

"You are the 'other' woman. You've been the other woman for a long time." Richard dropped his head. When he looked back up at me, there was an expression on his face I could not describe. It made me feel like the most loved woman in the world.

I was speechless. We just stared into each other's eyes.

"Felicia, say something. If you don't accept this man's proposal, I'm going to whup you. Shoot!" Grandma Lucy hollered. She and Richard laughed.

I blinked hard and swallowed a lump that had formed in my throat. "I don't know what to say," I bleated.

"Say something!" Grandma screeched. "Do it lickity-split so I can go to my bedroom in time to catch some of the *Family Feud* reruns."

"You can go on, Grandma Lucy. I'll come get you after I've had a few minutes alone with Richard."

CHAPTER 24

RICHARD

I had not planned to propose to Felicia in such a bizarre way. As a matter of fact, even after I'd purchased the ring I still had no clue how I was going to ask her, or when and where. If Grandma Lucy had not "intervened," I probably wouldn't have done it tonight. But I was glad I had.

After Grandma Lucy shuffled out of the room, grumbling under her breath and waving her arms, I slid the ring onto Felicia's finger again. She stifled a sob and stared at it for several moments. "It's too beautiful for words. It's exactly what I would have picked out for myself," she managed.

"You did," I reminded.

She leaned toward me and brushed her lips across my cheek. I pulled her into my arms and we kissed long and hard. It felt exactly the way I had imagined.

"That's more like it," I said with a sigh.

I took Felicia's hand and led her to the couch. I flopped down first and guided her into my lap. "I'm still in a state of shock," she said in a shy tone. "I . . . I had no idea you cared about me this way."

"Okay, I have to come clean." I paused and took a deep breath before I told her, "Pam told me what you told her."

Her jaw dropped and she covered her face with her hands. I took her hands in mine. "I . . . I'm so embarrassed," she whimpered. "I didn't know, I didn't mean . . . I knew I shouldn't have told her or anybody else how I felt about you." She let out an eerie laugh. "All those times you sat right beside me on the bus, and came to my office to work on my computer, it was so hard for me to keep such a deep dark secret from you."

"Why call it a 'deep dark secret'? Just a secret is all it was. Why didn't you save yourself some trouble and tell me?" I rolled my eyes and gave Felicia a sharp look. "Scratch that? I felt the same way and could have told you."

"When did you . . ."

"Realize I loved you? I'm not exactly sure, but it was quite a while ago."

She nodded. "Same here." We remained silent for a few moments. "When do you want to get married?" she asked.

"Baby, whenever you want to, we'll do it."

"Have you told your girls or anybody else?"

I shook my head. "I had to find out what you'd say first. I'll tell the girls when they come home tomorrow."

"I hope they'll be happy for you. You know how some kids feel about their parents remarrying. Especially to a woman they barely know."

"Believe me, my girls know enough about you. You'll all get along just fine." Richard chuckled. "Boy, I can't wait to tell my buddy Steven and Sam and the rest of the crew at work."

"Wait! You can tell your girls and the rest of your family and friends, but I don't want to share this with the folks at work yet. Pam and everybody else can wait."

"All right. When are you going to tell Clyde? Soon, I hope. I don't want him to ask you out again after today."

"If he asks me out before I tell him, I'll just turn him down. You know he's only just a friend anyway."

"So was I."

"You know what I mean."

"Okay, you share the news when you feel the

time is right. That's fine with me. Is there a reason you don't want to do it right away?"

She nodded. "Years ago, I told my mother that when and if I ever accepted a marriage proposal, she'd be the first to know. I'm going to try and get in touch with her tomorrow and tell her."

"You don't want to tell her in person?"

"I do, but I don't expect them back until after Christmas. I can't wait that long to let her know."

"Baby, you do whatever you have to do. I've waited this long, I can wait a few more weeks. Where are your parents today?"

"Still in Tokyo."

"I think they're thirteen hours ahead of us so it'd be midmorning Saturday there. Why don't you give her a call now?"

"Well, I can try, but knowing them they're probably out kicking up their heels. They spend very little time in their hotel rooms." Felicia was still in my lap when she leaned over and picked up a sheet of beige stationery off the end table. "It's a copy of their itinerary." She picked up the landline from the same table and dialed. It took a couple of minutes for her international call to go through. She pressed the speaker feature on the phone so I could hear both ends of the conversation.

"Hello, Mama."

There was a moment of hesitation on the

other end. "Fel, is everything all right?" a woman's husky voice finally asked.

Felicia let out a sharp laugh. "Everything is fine, Mama. I'm glad I caught you. Where's Daddy?"

"Standing here hovering over me like a hawk in a shirt that looks more like a kimono. Boris, don't you leave this room until you take your pill. He's about to go and try to play tennis again, with his clumsy self."

"Tell him to wait a few minutes. I have an important announcement to make."

"Uh-oh," Mrs. Hawkins said in a raspy tone. "Do I need to take one of my nerve pills first?"

"No, you don't," Felicia chuckled. "Remember when I promised you that you'd be the first to know when I accepted a marriage proposal?"

"Yeah. I'm still waiting."

"Well, the wait is over. I've accepted one."

There was a loud gasp on the other end. "Say what?"

"I'm engaged," Felicia said proudly as she held up her hand and gazed at her ring.

"Lord have mercy! Boris, our baby girl is finally getting married!"

Mr. Hawkins responded in a very jolly tone, "It sure took Clyde long enough to ask!"

Felicia immediately said, "It's not Clyde. It's someone else. I'm sure I've mentioned his name before, but you and Daddy have never met him.

We're coworkers and we've been friends for years."

"What's his name?" Mrs. Hawkins asked.

"Richard Grimes. And he's really nice, Mama. You and Daddy will love him. Grandma Lucy already does."

"You told her? I thought you said I'd be the first to know when you got engaged!" Mrs. Hawkins grumbled.

"I didn't exactly tell her. She figured it out on her own, but I didn't confirm anything. Technically, you're still the first to know because I didn't accept the proposal until Grandma Lucy left the room. I'll go tell her when I get off the phone."

"When are you going to get married? Daddy will have a hissy fit if he's not there to walk you down the aisle."

"I sure enough will," Mr. Hawkins confirmed.

"I hope you can wait until we get home," Mrs. Hawkins said. "If you can't, we'll cut the trip short and come home as soon as you want us to. We had hoped to visit the Holy Land on Christmas Day, but we can go visit it some other time. Even though our travel agent went to so much trouble to get us such a nice hotel and a guide. . . ."

"Don't you dare change your plans. You and Daddy have wanted to visit the Holy Land for years. You're too close to it to back out now. Besides, Richard and I haven't even discussed a date yet. But I'm sure it won't be before you and Daddy get back home." Felicia looked at me with her eyebrows raised and I nodded in agreement.

"Felicia, this is the best news since your birth. That young man has no idea what a prize he's getting. You're going to make a wonderful wife and mother."

"Well, Mama, I learned from the best. I'll let you and Daddy go and we'll talk again in a few days."

"Are you going to tell your brother, or do you want me to give him the news when I call him in a day or so?"

"I'll call him tomorrow. Now you two go on and have some more fun. Just be careful."

When Felicia hung up, I pulled her into my arms and kissed her again. When I released her, I reared back and stared into her eyes.

"What? What are you thinking? Why are you smiling like a cat that just swallowed a canary?" she asked.

"I never thought Christmas would come so early this year, and that I'd get the gift I wanted most of all."

"And the same goes for me," she replied.

CHAPTER 25
FELICIA

"Richard, I'm sorry I don't have any champagne in the house to make a toast," I said. Just as I was about to speak again, my landline rang. It was Lorena. "What's up?" I greeted.

"You tell me. Is he still there?" she whispered.

For my own amusement and for Richard's, I hit the speaker button for this call too.

I smothered a giggle. "Yes, he is."

"Whoever he is, he's been there quite a while . . ."

"He's spending the night," I explained.

"WHAT?"

"It's not what you think. He gave me a ride home from work. So many streets in this neighborhood are closed for I don't know how long, I told him he could spend the night." I looked at Richard and he winked.

"I know. I had a date coming over this evening and he had to cancel for the same reason. Anyway, I was looking out my window when you got here with him. He walks like a good man."

"I'm sure he is. Listen, I really can't talk now. I'll call you tomorrow."

"I'm going to sit by my phone until you do!"

I hung up and giggled. "How does a 'good man' walk?"

"Like me, I guess," Richard laughed.

I heard a noise in the hallway. When I turned around, Grandma Lucy was peeping around the corner. "You can come back out if you want to." She trotted over to us with a grin on her face. "I accepted the proposal," I stated proudly.

"Yaaaay!" She puckered her lips and kissed the top of my head. Then she shook Richard's hand. "By the way, there ain't never been no divorce in our family. Good night, y'all." Grandma Lucy did a jig-like shuffle out of the room, humming "Oh Happy Day," her favorite gospel tune.

Richard and I sat up all night. We talked about any and everything that entered our minds. One of the most important decisions we'd made was that I would move into his house after we exchanged vows. But the subject we discussed that was even more important was that we both wanted to have a child together as soon as possible. "Raising kids is not easy, but I wouldn't mind having at least a couple more," he admitted.

"I'd love even more," I said without hesitation.

During a lull in the conversation, Richard wrapped his arm around my shoulder. "Nobody is going to believe how our relationship developed."

"What do you mean?"

"Do you know how corny it was for me to ask you to help me pick out a ring for another woman instead of coming clean and letting you know everything from the get-go? It sounds like something you'd see in a Christmas TV movie on the Hallmark Channel."

I reared back and gasped. "*You* watch those movies?"

He nodded. "They're not the kind I usually watch, but my girls got hooked on them last year. I watch and record every new movie first to see if they are age-appropriate."

"Well, I've seen at least a dozen of those movies and I've never seen anything unsuitable for teenagers," I said firmly.

"I haven't either. I've even enjoyed a few," Richard admitted. We laughed. I'd done more laughing with him in the last few days than I'd done with everybody else in weeks. "You know, our story will give our friends, coworkers, and family something to talk about for years to come."

I gave him a thoughtful look. "We don't have to tell everybody the whole story. Especially how cat and mouse we acted before we finally revealed our feelings to each other."

"And if we tell them about the ring thing, we'll never hear the end of it. All they need to know is that we want to spend the rest of our lives together."

It was nine fifteen a.m. now. I had never gone without sleep for more than a whole day in my life and I wasn't the least bit sleepy. Enough snow had been cleared off the streets in my area for traffic to resume. After two cups of strong coffee and another passionate kiss, Richard left. I called Lorena back and told her everything. She squealed with delight and said hopefully, "Maybe I'm next."

I called up my brother and told him the news. He and his wife were ecstatic about it and couldn't wait to attend the wedding. I dialed Pam's number next. She was as dumbfounded as I was when I told her that I'd never suspected that the ring Richard wanted me to help him select was for me. "Fel, that's so romantic and original. When you told me he'd asked you to pick out an engagement ring for another woman, I didn't know what to make of it. But I never expected this." After she stopped giggling and expressing how happy my news had made her, I scolded her for telling Richard that I was in love with him.

"Oh, hush! Just like I told him, you didn't tell me *not* to!" she snapped. "And just think what might have happened if I hadn't. You and he might have gone to the grave still single. You ought to thank me."

"Pam, thank you."

"That's better."

Even with Grandma Lucy skittering about and jabbering away nonstop about things like the names for the children I planned to have and how often she could visit, I began to feel drowsy around ten o'clock. Before I could get up from the kitchen table where I'd eaten a bowl of oatmeal that Grandma Lucy had cooked, Richard called. "Hello, beautiful." Hearing him call me "beautiful" gave me goose bumps.

"Good morning," I said shyly. "I hope you didn't have too much trouble getting home."

"Aw, it was rough but I made it." He paused and I heard some mumbling in the background on his end. "My girls are here. Do you mind if I put on the speaker?"

"Not at all," I said quickly.

"Hello, Felicia. This is Marva."

"And Carol."

They sounded cheerful, but I could still feel my chest tighten. "Hello, girls. I guess your father broke the news about us."

"Yup! And it's about time," Marva chirped. "You'll really like him when you get to know him."

I was tempted to confess that I'd really liked him for years, but I saw no reason to go into that.

"Some nights he snores like a moose," Carol warned. "Mama used to wear earplugs when they went to bed. I'll buy you a bunch before the wedding."

"He's forgetful and he tells lame jokes," Marva tossed in.

"I don't know if I snore, but I'm forgetful and I tell lame jokes, too," I said with a lump in my throat. We all laughed. It pleased me to know that Richard's daughters were so receptive.

Richard and I spoke on the telephone several more times Saturday and Sunday. But when I woke up Monday morning, I wondered if I'd dreamed the whole thing. The beautiful ring on my finger squashed my concerns.

When I boarded the commuter bus Monday morning, Richard and Pam looked up at me with Cheshire cat grins on their faces as I sauntered down the aisle. "Hello, Mrs. Grimes," Pam started with a familiar mischievous expression on her face.

"Don't jump the gun. I'm not there yet," I told her. I flopped down beside Richard, bumping his knee with mine. "Hi," I said to him.

"Hello, *Mrs. Grimes*," he said in a low voice. I almost melted into the seat.

It was an interesting week. We had planned to announce our engagement at the Christmas luncheon, but by nine a.m. almost everybody had heard the news. Coworkers swarmed into my office like locusts to congratulate me. Even the young secretaries who had been flirting with Richard for years. "We were wondering when you two would get together," Sandy gushed. She stood in the doorway of my office with Marybeth and Ramona in tow. Three other coworkers had left a few minutes earlier.

I did a double take. "What made you girls think Richard and I were going to get together?" I asked, looking from one face to another.

"Come on, boss lady. We're not blind. I've never seen a man look at a woman the way Richard looks at you!" Ramona hollered.

"I don't know about the rest of our coworkers, but we knew it was just a matter of time before you and Richard got serious," Marybeth chimed in. "You two were made for each other."

I heard similar comments the rest of the week.

Our office Christmas luncheon was a big hit. We'd ordered more than enough Chinese, Italian, and soul food to accommodate the ninety people who showed up. But it didn't take long before every single container was empty.

At every office event, Sam would encourage people to share any information they thought their coworkers would like to know. One of the technicians Richard supervised raised his hand and literally ran to the podium at the front of the room. He revealed that he'd be transferring to the home office in February. The job Richard had turned down had been offered to him and he had accepted it immediately. One of the trainers announced that his son had recently passed the bar exam. A secretary in the payroll department shared the news that she was in the process of purchasing her first home.

"I'm sure everybody already knows, but do you still want to go up and formally announce our engagement?" I whispered in Richard's ear. We occupied a spot in the back of the room.

"Of course!" he answered, bobbing his head to an instrumental version of "Joy to the World" playing in the background.

When the secretary finished sharing her news, Richard and I held hands and started to inch forward. But before we could plow through the crowd, Sam trotted up to the podium. "I'm sure you'll all love to hear what I have to say." He rolled his eyes up and cleared this throat. "This year, our office will be closed for the whole week of Christmas, starting with Christmas Eve. That'll be my gift to you all." Nobody reacted until they heard what he said next. "And all five days off will be with pay." People whistled, cheered, and stomped like they were at a rodeo. Sam was beaming like a lighthouse. He rambled on a few more minutes about things of no interest to anyone except himself. When he finally stopped talking, he looked directly at Richard and me and asked, "Do we have any other announcements?" By now, almost everybody present was fidgeting and checking the time.

"Over here!" Richard yelled. We held hands and skittered up to the podium. "Felicia and I are getting married next year." The crowd cheered even louder this time. Then Richard hauled off and kissed me like I'd never been kissed before.

EPILOGUE

RICHARD

December 25

Felicia quickly became my daughters' newest best friend. Marva and Carol couldn't believe that I was going to marry a woman they thought was "real cool" and so pretty. They had helped her prepare the meal we'd planned for a few of our relatives and friends to celebrate our engagement and the holiday today.

Felicia and I had decided to get married in April next year. As picture-postcard beautiful as Ohio was in the wintertime, it was never a good time to get married. My brother's wedding had occurred in December. Half the people on the guest list had not been able to make it because of the severe weather conditions that day.

Felicia didn't want a big church wedding and that was fine with me. Had we been ten or fifteen years younger, I would have thought differently. We agreed to exchange vows in my living room. My house was where the dozen people we'd invited would gather today in less than a couple of hours. Marva and Carol were in their room enjoying a video chat with their grandparents. My former in-laws had previously planned to spend the holiday with other relatives. Otherwise, they would have been in the house long before now. They were as happy for us as everybody else.

Despite the fact that Pam had cooked up a feast and had guests coming to her own house later in the day, she and her husband and two of their grandchildren had already arrived two hours early. He was in the living room with the grandkids watching game shows and Pam was in the kitchen with Felicia and me.

"Felicia, I'm glad you didn't want to get married before Marybeth and Ramona. They were so afraid that if you did, all our coworkers' attention would be on you," Pam said. She and I and Felicia were at my kitchen table. There was an empty eggnog carton on the table in front of us. We'd drunk two glasses each.

"I can understand why they'd feel that way," Felicia replied. "A girl's wedding is a big deal, especially at their ages. Some older people like us don't want their wedding to be too elaborate."

"Speaking of older people, guess who else is going to get married?" Pam piped in, bouncing up and down in her chair. She looked like she was going to burst wide open if she didn't get the information out fast enough.

I didn't waste any time asking, "Who?"

"Clyde is going to marry that woman in Cleveland he's been seeing!" Felicia exclaimed.

"Pffftt! Not hardly," Pam responded with a dismissive wave. "That boy has it too easy living at home. But now that it's happening for you two, there's hope for him."

"Then who is it, Pam?" I asked. I was so antsy I could barely stand still.

"Regina."

"Regina?" I boomed. I had seen her out and about several times since our dim sum lunch. We'd been cordial to each other, but each time she'd rushed away from me within seconds. Despite how she felt about me now, I would always consider her a friend.

"Who is she going to marry?" Felicia asked.

"A used-car salesman she met online last year. They dated off and on, and he helped her find a car to replace her old one. Last week they finally decided to get engaged. When I was at Macy's on Saturday, I ran into the young intern who works with Regina. Susan told me that, and she said Regina couldn't be happier."

"I'm happy for her," I admitted. And I was.

"Felicia, your mama's on the telephone," Carol yelled from the living room. Felicia jumped up out of her chair and grabbed the extension above the counter.

"Mama!" She didn't speak again for about half a minute. And then her eyes got big and her mouth dropped open. "Is it everything you thought it would be?" A few more moments of silence passed. "I'm so glad to hear that, Mama. Tell Daddy to enjoy himself. And please take plenty of pictures." She covered the mouthpiece with her hand and said with her voice shaking, "My folks made it to the Holy Land today." She listened for a couple more minutes and when she hung up there were tears in her eyes. "This is the best Christmas I've ever had."

"I feel the same way," I said.

DISCUSSION QUESTIONS

1. If you loved someone from afar, do you think you'd ever let that person know your true feelings?

2. Do you think Pam was out of line by telling Richard that Felicia was in love with him?

3. Do you have any busybody friends like Pam? If so, are they just as harmless and comical?

4. If you had a secret admirer and someone told you, would you let your admirer know you knew?

5. When Felicia told Pam how she felt about Richard, she didn't tell her not to tell him. Pam was a blabbermouth, so she couldn't keep it to herself. If a friend told you something personal that involved another person and *didn't* tell you to keep it to yourself, would you?

6. Felicia had a great relationship with her meddlesome, fussy grandmother and was

very patient with her. What are your relationships with elderly people like?

7. Regina frequently "bumped into" Richard in public. It was obvious that she was trying to have a more serious relationship with him. Richard was always nice to her, even when he didn't want to be in her presence. Were you happy when he finally told her that they would never have a future together?

8. Felicia and Richard always looked on the bright side of things. When Felicia thought Richard was going to marry another woman, she didn't get jealous. She was happy for him. How would you feel in the same situation?

9. If someone you were secretly in love with asked you to help them pick out an engagement ring for them to give someone else, would you?

10. It's nice to be "just friends" with a member of the opposite sex. But do you have any male/female friends in your life you'd like to be more than friends with?

11. For most people Christmas is a spiritual and joyful time. Was this an uplifting story to you because of when it takes place?

12. Would this story have had the same effect if it had occurred during a different holiday?

13. Richard was an excellent father. But do you think he was a little too strict with his daughters?

Embrace the holiday spirit with these
Uplifting, heartwarming stories from
Mary Monroe
REMEMBRANCE
THE GIFT OF FAMILY
And
Keep reading for a sneak peek at
The latest delightful story
ONCE IN A LIFETIME
Available now from
Dafina Books

When I got up at eight a.m. Saturday morning, rain was thumping on the windows of my second-floor apartment like little rocks. That was one of the reasons I was still in my bathrobe and slippers two hours later when somebody knocked on my front door. I assumed it was one of my neighbors in the building because anybody else would have called before coming, and I would have had to buzz them in.

I looked through the peephole and saw a face I didn't recognize. One thing I never did was open my door to a stranger: male or female, day or night. I'd read about people who had done that and been pepper-sprayed, attacked, robbed, or all three. "Who is it?" I used the same curt tone I used when I had to deal with pesky tele-marketers and overly aggressive salespeople. It never failed to discourage them.

"I'm looking for Vanessa Hayes," came the meek reply.

"What is this regarding?"

"I came to deliver a piece of her mail that the mailman accidentally left in my mailbox."

I slowly opened the door. Standing in front of me was a slim woman who appeared to be in her early forties. She had long, thick, black hair, and small brown eyes on a honey-colored face. Despite the weary look in her eyes and the dark circles underneath them, she was still pretty. "I'm Vanessa Hayes," I said in a much softer tone.

"I hope I'm not disturbing you," the woman said, looking me up and down. She wore an expensive-looking beige pants suit underneath a see-through raincoat, and she was holding a large umbrella.

"No, you didn't."

"I don't know when your mail was left in my mailbox. I had to go out of town for three weeks and just returned last night." She smiled and reached into her denim purse and pulled out a large white envelope and handed it to me. "I had put in a request at the post office for them to hold my mail, but they still sent something through that doesn't even belong to me."

I immediately noticed the official-looking return address. "This must be my passport! I applied for it weeks ago!" I exclaimed. I didn't know why I was standing in my doorway on a rainy Saturday morning telling a total stranger my business. Since she looked like she was interested, I kept talking. "I was going to reapply, but I was told that I probably wouldn't receive it in time for my vacation next month."

The woman sighed and shook her head. "Hopefully, you can still go now."

I shook my head. "I've already canceled my travel arrangements."

"I'm sorry to hear that. Anyway, I'll be on my way—"

I held up my hand. "Wait. Let me give you gas money for bringing this to me."

"No, that's not necessary," she said, shaking her head. "I have a few other errands to take care of today, so it was no problem." Then she gave me a puzzled look. "What I don't understand is how your mail ended up in my area. I have received other folks' mail before, but they all live on my street or close by. I was surprised to see something for someone who resides on Alice Street."

"Where do you live?"

"Webb Street."

"That's on the other side of town."

"I'm sorry I couldn't get it to you in time for your vacation." The woman gave me another smile and turned to leave.

"Um, what's your name? I really appreciate your thoughtfulness and would love to compensate you in some way."

"My name is Judith Ann Guthrie-Starks." She chuckled. "I know that's a mouthful, but I didn't want to give up my daddy's name just because I got married. He was from the UK and a lot of the women over there hyphenate their last names, married or not."

"That's interesting. Is that where you're from?"

"No, it's not. My father's family moved to London from Jamaica when he was a child. The company he worked for transferred him to California. My brother and I were born here. However, when we were children we spent every summer in London with my uncle and his family. It's a wonderful place and I have a lot of family and friends still there."

"My mother used to work for an airline, and she loved her stopovers in London." I was really enjoying this impromptu conversation, so I went on. "As much as she enjoyed her job, she retired five years ago so she could spend more time with my father. He'd already retired a couple of years before."

Judith tilted her head to the side and chuckled. "What a coincidence. My mother was a flight attendant for fifteen years. When my father died two years ago, she moved back to London. She passed last year."

"I'm sorry for your loss. Would you like to come in for a cup of coffee?" I felt comfortable and wanted to chat some more. The rain had made me feel gloomy, so this was a welcome diversion. I opened the door wider and motioned for Judith to enter.

"No, thank you!" she exclaimed, shaking her head. "I have a busy day planned, so I really must be going. Good day."

Before I could say another word, Judith spun around and padded down the hall.

The second I closed the door, my landline rang. It was Madeline. "You ignored the message I left on your cell phone last night," she accused.

"Sorry. I went to visit my folks after I got off work. It was kind of late when I got home."

"I would give anything in the world to have my folks closer. It's hard to believe they moved to Florida three years ago," Madeline said with a heavy sigh. But her tone perked up so quickly, it startled me. "Kirk is taking the kids to Berkeley to spend some time with his folks, so I'm at loose ends. Let's go shopping. We can have lunch and get our nails done, too."

"I don't want to go out in this nasty weather. I just got over a cold," I said as I plopped down on the couch.

"Okay, but don't get mad when you hear about all the nice pieces I picked up today. That boutique on Willow Street is having a going-out-of-business sale and I want to get there before all the good stuff is gone."

"I don't need any new clothes. I have items in my closet with the tags still attached from the numerous going-out-of-business sales we've been to this year. If you find something I like, I can always borrow it from you, like I always do," I chuckled. I cleared my throat. "Listen, I just had an interesting encounter."

"Please tell me Barry hasn't had a change of heart and now wants—"

I cut Madeline off. "My passport ended up in another woman's mailbox and she just delivered it."

"So? What's so interesting about that? My neighbors' mail ends up in my box from time to time, and vice versa."

"The odd thing is, this woman lives across town on Webb Street. You've been supervising mail processing at the post office for five years. Do they make mistakes like this often?"

"Everybody makes mistakes. Even us postal workers," Madeline said, sounding slightly defensive. "But your mail being delivered so far away is odd. It's the first time I've ever heard of something like this happening. Well, at least you received your passport in time for your vacation."

"I didn't think I would, so I canceled it on Monday. I'll have to visit Paris some other time."

Madeline took her time responding. "V, what if that mail mix-up wasn't a mistake and your passport was supposed to end up with that woman?"

"That's ridiculous. Why would that be?"

"Well, they say everything happens for a reason."

"You sound like Mama. That's one of her favorite sayings."

"Maybe you *had* to cancel because something more important is going to happen in your life that you need to be here for."

"Well, whatever it is, I can't wait for it to happen."